from
alice to Zen
and everyone in Between

Chapter One

"Breakfast, Alice Bunt!"

My father, Jim Bunt, called me from the kitchen of our brand-new, 3,500-square-foot white colonial house. It was our first morning waking up in the suburbs.

"Breakfast, Sophie Bunt!"

Now he was calling my mother, who had to make the 7:30 train into Boston. She was the vice president of marketing at the largest book publisher in New England.

"Breakfast, Einstein and Yaz Bunt!"

Those two were my dog and cat. Einstein was supposedly the smartest pug puppy his breeder had ever sold. And my tabby cat was named after my all-time fave baseball player, Carl "Yaz" Yastrzemski.

All four of us rushed down the wide stairs into the foyer through the long living room past the cathedral dining room and into the kitchen with its seven-foot windows looking out over the half-acre lawn.

Wow, our new house was enormous!

You have to understand, for the past eleven years of my life—my whole life—we had lived in a small apartment in Boston. There was my teeny bedroom, one tiny bathroom, Mom and Pop's little bedroom, and one large everything room. That was it. We did all our living in that large everything room: cooked, ate, played, talked, worked, and watched TV.

"Smells delicious, dear," remarked my mother as she sat at the head of the kitchen table. "How are the new appliances?"

"Work like a charm!" Pop, beaming.

Einstein and Yaz were happily gobbling up their morning chow.

"Ooh, Pop, my fave!" I exclaimed. "Rocket waffles."

My dad was an expert at making waffles. His secret ingredient was powdered sugar. Once, when I was very young, he cut the waffles into the shape of a rocket to get me to try them. He's been doing it ever since.

Mom checked her watch, then slipped on her suit

jacket. "I wish I had time for one more. They're so delicious."

"I have time for a hundred more!" I announced.

My mother playfully swatted my head with the morning paper. "So what are your plans today, dear?"

"You'll have to keep busy, Al," said Pop. "I have loads to unpack."

I had plenty to do. I was in a new house with a new yard in a newly built neighborhood. In fact, we were the first family to settle in. Three other houses, exactly like ours, had also been constructed on this cul-de-sac at the end of Hemlock Trail.

"Didn't you say the people in the tan house were moving in this afternoon?" I asked.

My father placed another steaming rocket waffle on my plate.

"That's right," he answered, pointing his spatula toward the window. "I believe their last name is Reed."

"I *so* hope they have a kid my age!"

I was really excited about the idea of running from house to house, yard to yard. In the city, I had felt a little trapped, as if we lived in a giant people crate. And either Mom or Pop had to walk me to the park daily, the same way I walked Einstein and Yaz. The city was just too busy for me to explore alone.

"I'm sure between those three houses," said Pop, "there's bound to be at least one other child around eleven years old."

Mom stood up and cleared her plate. She pecked my father on the cheek, then leaned over my head. I loved the flowery smell of her linen suit and blow-dried hair.

"Have a wonderful day, dear," she said, kissing the tips of my ears. "And say hello to everyone you meet!"

"Well, *don't* say hello to the city," I teased. "I don't miss it one bit!"

Einstein licked the floor around my slippers, vacuuming up waffle crumbs. Yaz perched by one of the huge windows, stalking birds or something beyond the yard. It was almost 90 degrees outside, and it might reach 100 by the end of the day, a real heat wave. But we had air-conditioning.

This life was going to be pretty perfect.

The morning flew by. First, I introduced Einstein and Yaz to every room in the house. Then we pulled apart our Fave Box, which I had packed in the apartment for the three of us to open up in the new house. I knew it would take a long time to unpack every carton, so I put together one box of our favorite things.

We settled down in the carpeted rec room. It was located in the basement and stretched the entire length of the house. The Fave Box contained Einstein's rubber clown, which he liked to carry in his mouth most of the day. It also had Yaz's cloth snake, which he dragged by the tail, then occasionally attacked. And I had two favorites: my pop's old baseball mitt, signed by the best left fielder in the whole world (C.Y.), and my uncle's old Erector Set. It had tons of connecting metal slats and screws and even a motor that still worked.

Before I knew it, I had built a miniature Eiffel Tower and lunch was ready.

"Shall we eat in the dining room or out on the patio, Mademoiselle?" asked Pop, imitating a fancy waiter.

"Or would you prefer the counter?"

My father was kind of a stay-at-home dad. I say "kind of" because he had a job, but he could do it anywhere. He bought old stuff at yard sales or through the newspaper and then sold it for a whole lot more on the Internet. In fact, that's how we got the down payment for this house. Last fall, Pop discovered a book that President John F. Kennedy himself had signed. Pop bought it for sixty dollars at a flea market in Maine and sold it for sixty *thousand* to some guy in Arkansas.

"Looks like the truck is early," said my dad. He took a sip of chocolate milk.

Through the bay window in the dining room, I watched Huff and Puff Movers navigate carefully around the cul-de-sac. They stopped in front of the tan 3,500-square-foot colonial house, number 3. A minivan with New Jersey plates pulled up behind the truck. Einstein began snorting and yapping as Yaz leapt up onto the windowsill, ready to pounce if necessary.

"Thanks for the veggie wrap, Pop. May I be excused?"

My father grinned. "Invite the whole Reed family

over for dessert tonight, Al. I'll bake my world-famous triple-chocolate brownies!"

I snapped leashes on Einstein and Yaz, then charged out into the steamy air. At first I felt woozy. I had forgotten that I was living in air-conditioning, so the heat of the summer came as a shock. Einstein stopped in front of me and whimpered.

"I'm not getting the stroller, you big baby. You need the exercise."

Einstein hated walking outside, partly because pugs don't breathe too well, but also because of my old baby stroller. When Einstein was a puppy, I used to push him around in it. He even wore my old sunbonnet. The problem was, he never outgrew the stroller and still preferred being pushed in it. Mom had planned to give it away before we moved, but I convinced her to hang onto it until Einstein adjusted to his new surroundings.

The three of us plopped down on the curb and stared at the new family. Yaz pulled at his leash, so I held him on my lap. A mother and father got out of the car. I wasn't sure, but it seemed like their clothes matched on purpose. They both wore a white shirt with green shorts. The two of them held hands as they strolled over to the front door of the house.

Suddenly the mother noticed me and waved excitedly. I stood up and tugged Einstein, who immediately started his snorting. Yaz leapt ahead, pouncing this way and that as if he was killing every ant in the street.

"Are we neighbors?" asked the father. He bent over to pet Einstein, who licked the man's arm like it was made out of mayonnaise.

"We're in the white one," I answered. "Number 1."

"You beat us here," the woman giggled. "We're the Reeds, Bill and Sue."

"We're the Bunts. I'm Alice and this is Einstein and that's Yaz."

"Do you and your pets live alone, Miss Bunt?" Mr. Reed joked.

"My parents are Jim and Sophie. Oh, and my dad said you should all stop over for dessert later tonight." I attempted to peer through the shaded minivan windows, then asked, "So where are your kids?"

The Reeds chuckled and gazed at each other, the way people do on television when they've just gotten married.

"Our first one's on the way, Alice," said Mrs. Reed, patting her normal-sized belly. "By then, you might be old enough to be a mother's helper."

Have I mentioned I can't stand baby kids? They pester you with annoying questions and then they want you to play the dumbest games that were ever invented. Like once, my three-year-old cousin Daniel spent the whole day at our apartment in the bathtub without any water. I had to sit on the floor and call out, "Tugboat Daniel, coming through!" as he slid down the back of the tub and blew his whistle. For the *whole day*.

"Any pets?" I asked hopefully.

"Nope, we're too darn busy," Mr. Reed grinned. "We both work in the city. How else are we gonna afford this mansion?"

Then they broke out into hysterics. I didn't see what was so funny. If they thought a pet was a lot of work, wait until they had a kid.

chapter two

The day after Mr. and Mrs. Reed moved in (and later stopped over for brownies), another moving van drove up Hemlock Trail and steered slowly around the cul-de-sac. Valuable Van Lines stopped at the pale gray 3,500-square-foot colonial house, number 2, next door to us. Not a minute later a minivan tore up the street, slamming on the brakes just inches from the back of the truck.

I blasted out of the house onto the front lawn, then stopped just as fast.

"That's the last time, young man!" the father hollered as he stepped out of the passenger side. "No more driving until I take some lead out of that foot!"

The teenager in the driver's seat ignored his father and continued revving the engine like he was a racecar driver. Then a round lady with red hair climbed out of the back seat.

"Don't be so dramatic, Bob!" Her voice was loud and scratchy like a parrot's. "You're an excellent driver, Travis. Don't listen to your father."

"For Pete's sake, Marian, you're just encouraging him!"

I decided I didn't want to get into the middle of this family squabble. So I scooped up Einstein and grabbed Yaz, who was creeping down the driveway, and quietly snuck back toward our house. I didn't even wait to see if there was another kid my age.

"Yoo-hoo, next-door neighbor!" Marian shrieked.

I politely turned around to say hello, and that's when I noticed the tiny Chihuahua she was carrying under her plump arm.

"Oh, your dog is so cute!" I rushed over, still lugging Einstein and Yaz.

All of a sudden Marian thrust her other arm out, commanding me to halt.

"Don't come any closer with those animals!" she yelled loud enough for the Reeds to hear. "Kissy-Missy is worth over two thousand dollars and she's shaking like a leaf."

Her husband approached me, laughing awkwardly, as I slowly backed toward my front door. The teenager turned the car radio up even louder and croaked out a song.

"Bob, Marian, and Travis Lee!" the husband shouted. "Delaware!"

"I'm Alice Bunt and this is Einstein and that's Yaz," I replied as I retreated up the steps. "My mom, Sophie, works in Boston and my pop, Jim, asked me to invite you over for dessert later tonight. Bye!" I yelped and quickly closed the door.

They came over for dessert all right and brought that yapping Kissy-Missy. In fact, Marian insisted that I banish Yaz and Einstein to another room so that her precious Chihuahua would stop trembling. And then she served Kissy-Missy an itty-bitty slice of raspberry cheesecake and even wiped her snout with a cloth napkin. Travis never said a word. Instead he slumped down in the corner on the floor and played with his handheld video game the entire hour.

The next day wasn't much better. In fact, it was worse.

"I'm almost afraid to look," I said to Pop as I hid behind the curtains in the dining room.

The last truck, Home Again Movers, had just pulled up to the cream-colored 3,500-square-foot colonial house, number 4. Two matching minivans pulled into the driveway. My father was in the kitchen rolling a piecrust for tonight's dessert guests, the third and final family.

"I'm sure they're just as—" Pop paused to find the right word—"*interesting* as the Reeds and the Lees."

Up until that point, I hadn't totally given up on this cul-de-sac neighborhood. It was still possible that a fun family would move in, perhaps with a kid my age. Who knows, the kid could even end up liking the same stuff I did, like sports and construction kits and video games and, of course, animals. We could even be best friends.

"There's a girl getting out of each car," I reported from behind the curtain to my father in the kitchen.

"No, *two* girls out of each car!"

"How old?" asked Pop. "Anyone around eleven?"

I scanned the group frantically as a total of six people—a mom, a dad, and their daughters—jumped out onto the driveway.

"Oh no, they're all little. And they look exactly alike!"

My dad hurried over to the window. "What do you mean?"

I watched in horror as four identical girls, about five years old, ran in manic circles around the moving van, whacking the poor movers with their dolls each time they raced by.

"How do you like that? Quadruplets!" exclaimed Pop. "Ask them if they'd like to come over for blueberry pie. On second thought, I better make another."

"*You* ask them," I moaned in total despair.

Not one kid even close to eleven years old on the whole cul-de-sac.

Einstein, Yaz, and I descended the stairs to the rec room and, reluctantly, resumed playing with the plastic clown, stuffed snake, baseball mitt, and Erector Set.

It looked like this life wasn't going to be perfect after all.

Dessert with the Kings was so horrible, I can barely talk about it. I can tell you that all four girls enjoyed harassing older kids like me and had absolutely zero experience handling pets like Einstein and Yaz.

For example, when I helped my mother that night by carrying the two blueberry pies from the kitchen to the living room, my hands were obviously full. The quadruplets surrounded me and attacked. Jenni stuck gum on my back, Jessi stuffed ice in my pocket, Juli shoved a Band-Aid in my hair, and Jacki scribbled on my arm with a purple pen. Soon after, Jenni and Jessi fed peppermints to Einstein from the candy dish while Juli and Jacki wrapped Yaz in cocktail napkins.

And their parents were the type who thought everything they did was so funny and adorable. I could tell even patient Pop was growing impatient.

The following morning (a Saturday), as Mom, Pop, and I vacuumed and swept and scrubbed up the consequences of having the Kings over, I collapsed onto the floor.

"This neighborhood stinks."

My parents stopped cleaning simultaneously.

"Don't say that, Al," said Pop. "You have to give it time."

Mom added, "We barely know these people, dear."

Yaz climbed lightly onto my stomach and curled up into a ball. Einstein, not to be left out, crossed his paws over my shoulder.

"Believe me," I said, "I know enough. The Reeds are dull, the Lees are rude, and the Kings are a nightmare! And not one kid my age . . . "

Mom and Pop sat on the couch and peered down over my face. They both seemed perplexed. I knew that it had never occurred to them that this could actually be worse than living in the city. I mean, after all, we now owned a huge house with a gigantic lawn on a real suburban cul-de-sac.

"Alice, dear? Why don't you take a walk?" suggested Mom.

Pop grinned. "That's a wonderful idea, Sophie."

I sat up and asked, "A walk? Where?"

"Down the street," said Mom.

"Yes," agreed Pop. "Take a right *or* a left at the end of Hemlock Trail and see who else lives in Oakville."

"But take your cell phone," said Mom.

"And your safety whistle," remembered Pop. "Oh, and a list of emergency numbers."

"They should be programmed into her cell phone," said Mom to Pop.

A walk? By myself? Wandering around and venturing down other blocks had never been an option for me in the city. I only knew the few people in our building and Marky Dukakis in the duplex two doors down. I visited my friends from school, but I never would have walked up and down streets looking for people to meet.

"Should I take Einstein and Yaz?"

Mom and Pop glanced up from my cell phone.

"You should probably leave them here and scope it out first," replied Pop.

Ten minutes later, my parents were waving to me as

if I were leaving for good. In my backpack I had the preprogrammed cell phone and safety whistle, in addition to snacks, a bottle of water, money, suntan lotion, hand wipes, and my fave baseball mitt. Pop held Yaz, who was squirming to follow me, and Einstein looked a little sad standing in the doorway.

I felt great marching off down the road leaving the cul-de-sac behind me. For the first time in my life I was completely free. My strides were long and perfectly equal. I was on my own and didn't have a clue where I was going. I even whistled as I walked around the bend and the four identical houses disappeared.

This life was going to be pretty wonderful after all.

Up ahead, the stop sign marked my first big decision: Would I turn left or right? And that's when I met Zenithal Stevie Wonder Malinowski.

Chapter three

"Are you running away already?"

Around the corner to the left of the stop sign, a big, bulky boy sat in a ratty lounge chair under the thick shade of an old tree. His hair was so blond it looked white. And it was unusually curly. He wore a hand-painted T-shirt and cut-off jeans exposing the palest legs I had ever seen. In his right hand, he held a magazine, and in his left, a glass of lemonade with a bendy straw.

"Don't you like Hemlock*less* Trail?"

I stopped and stared, not sure if I should talk to him.

"Isn't it clever how the builders named the road after the very trees they cut down?"

I glanced back up the street, but I had no idea what a hemlock tree would look like.

"So didn't you people just move into your cookie-cutter chateau? Which one is yours?"

I finally replied, "The white one."

"Oooh, aren't you lucky!" he squeaked. "However, I would have preferred the tan one. Tan is *sooo* much more interesting than white."

I peered over at his house. It was a small box, probably not much bigger than our old apartment. The green paint was peeling, and one of the four yellow shutters was broken. The whole front yard was heavily shaded by the enormous tree that he was sitting under. So there wasn't any grass, only dirt. In the driveway a beat-up black Volkswagen Bug (the old-fashioned kind) was backed up against a shed.

"Want some lemonade before you run away?" he offered.

"I'm not running away."

"I wouldn't blame you if you did," he said. He stood and pulled at his shorts. When he turned around I saw that he had red chair marks on the back of his chubby, pale legs. "Now stay right there and I'll get the lemonade."

Maybe the Reeds, the Lees, and the Kings weren't so

bad if this was what the rest of Oakville was like. I glanced down the street but saw no other homes, just trees.

"I hope you like lots of ice," said the boy as he returned with another glass.

The metal screen door banged as it closed behind him. I noticed he was tall and heavy, but I mostly noticed that his whole body hurried when he walked.

I set down my backpack. "Thank you."

On the other side of the old tree was a dirty beach chair. He pulled it over and set it in front of me.

"So what's your name?"

"Alice."

"That's it?" he asked. He dropped down onto his chair like he was fifty years old and stirred the ice in his glass. "That's not much of a name."

I slowly sat down on the filthy beach chair, giving it a quick brush beforehand.

"Alice Bunt is my whole name."

The boy thought for a moment, then said, "A monosyllabic surname, but I like it. It's short and to the point. How old are you, Alice Bunt?"

"Eleven."

"No!" he replied quickly.

"Yes I am," I answered defensively. I was used to people challenging me about my age. I knew I was small, and I guess I seemed young too.

"Well, I can tell you," he said seriously, "you are going to be the littlest thing at Sachem Regional Middle School."

I frowned and wondered if that was true. Back in the city, two girls and one boy in my grade were a bit smaller than me. I wasn't used to being the very shortest one.

"Did you used to go to the middle school?" I asked.

The boy laughed so hard he snorted. Lemonade came up though his nose. He ran into the house, coughing and laughing. *Slam* went the door. He hurried back with a box of tissues. *Slam*. He dabbed his eyes and settled back into his lounge chair.

"I apologize. I overreacted," he said. "No, I've never gone to the middle school, Alice, but I will in the fall like you. Maybe we'll be in some classes together."

I almost dropped my drink.

"You're eleven?"

"Technically twelve. I stayed back in third grade 'cause I was sick for five months."

"What were you sick with for so long?"

"School-*itis*. My grandmother was in the hospital for five months, so I didn't bother to go to school. No one really noticed."

I didn't understand. "If my grandmother is sick, I still have to go to school."

"But I *live* with Babs and only Babs."

"Babs?"

"My grandmother, *Babcia*," the boy groaned. He was speaking faster and faster, as if his mouth was getting warmed up. "It's Polish for grandmother. But I call her Babs for short. It's catchier, don't you think?"

Just then my cell phone rang *Take Me Out to the Ball Game*. I quickly unzipped the outside pocket of my backpack.

"Is that a Quotarola X88 Ultimate LAZR in starburst

silver?" he asked.

"Yep and it's my pop." I flipped open the phone.

"Hi Al, how's it going?" my dad inquired.

"Okay."

"Met anyone yet? Your mother wants to know."

I glanced up at the boy and realized I didn't know his name. He was in the middle of tearing pages from his magazine, then neatly placing them in a folder on the dusty ground under his chair.

"Yeah Pop, I took a left at the stop sign and met a kid who lives around the corner at the end of our street." I covered the cell phone and whispered, "What's your name?"

The boy whispered back, "Zenithal Stevie Wonder Malinowski."

"Huh?" I needed him to repeat all four names.

The boy sighed. "Just call me Zen."

Even though he was a neighbor around my age, I wasn't sure if I wanted to get to know Zen any better. So I told him that I had to get going. I zipped up my backpack and thanked him for the lemonade. He took my glass and told me to stop over anytime. Then he went back to tearing pages out of his magazine.

I practically jogged down Zen's street so I'd look like I was late and had somewhere important to go. After a moment I glanced back to see if he was watching me, but the lounge chair was empty and Zen was gone.

I slowed down and kicked at a rock. I didn't know what to think of Zeni-something Stevie Walter Maloney or whatever he was called. What a strange name and what a strange kid. He even spoke in a peculiar way, like he had only thirty seconds to say a hundred things.

After about a quarter mile of trees, I finally passed a few homes, mostly small ones like Zen's, but in much better shape. A baby kid waved from a swing, but as I said before, I don't really like little kids.

Within a few minutes, I arrived at a river about as wide as first base to left field. I didn't remember my parents mentioning a river. The temperature was on the rise again, another scorcher by the afternoon. So I stepped out to the end of a dock, slipped out of my sandals, and sat down. My feet tingled in the cool water. I realized I had never done anything like this before, except when we were on vacation.

"It's private, but nobody cares."

I twisted around. There was Zen, holding a striped umbrella with the words *BODY BY DESIGN* printed along the bottom. He had changed into orange pants and sneakers and was out of breath.

"The dock, I mean," he explained. "Old Man Weagan owns it, but he doesn't even bother to yell at people anymore. He's just too old to care, like Babs."

He hurried as he walked down the dock, sticking his free arm out to balance himself.

"It's more than ninety degrees and sunny," I said. "Why do you have an umbrella?"

"Allergic to the sun," Zen sighed. "It's very inconvenient."

I had never heard of anyone being allergic to the sun. It was like being allergic to water.

Zen made all kinds of squeaks and grunts as he plopped down next to me. He asked me to hold his umbrella while he carefully took off each sneaker and rolled up his pants.

"Oh, isn't that refreshing," he said as he dipped his feet into the river.

"Want your umbrella back?"

"Yes, thank you, Alice," he answered politely and smiled.

His hair smelled awfully good, like cinnamon and roses mixed together. Up close I could see that he had very blue eyes and long eyelashes. He was quite overweight, and his pale skin was as smooth as the inside of a shell.

I had no idea what to say to him, so I finally asked, "What's your whole name again?"

He studied his hand and counted off each name on a different finger.

"Zen is short for Zenithal, which is my spiritual name. It means *at or near the zenith*, the highest point, the apex."

He stuck up his third and fourth fingers.

"Stevie Wonder is obvious. He was signed as a mere

child by Berry Gordy at Motown Records in 1961 and is considered to be the country's premiere R&B singer-songwriter of all time."

Then he lifted his pinky.

"And Malinowski is my mother's last name, because I don't have a father. That is, my mother has no idea exactly who he would be and so far, no one's come forward."

That last statement made Zen laugh really hard. He kicked at the water with his toes.

"I thought you said you only lived with your grandmother."

"Indeed I do. My mother abandoned me when I was three years old."

"Abandoned you!" I was shocked. "Where did she go?"

Zen blew a long, slow breath.

"At first to attend a Stevie Wonder concert at the Hollywood Bowl out in California. But there was a terrible thunderstorm, which was rare for that time of year, and the concert was canceled. Babs saw it on the news." Then he added casually, "But ever since then, we haven't heard a word from Mother."

One thing was obvious to me. Zen was very bored. The fact that he'd bothered to change his clothes, venture into the sun, follow me, then tell me his life's story all within fifteen minutes was proof enough. But then he practically admitted it.

"Where did you move from, Alice?"

"The city."

"Boston?" He cringed. "Oh you poor thing!"

"What do you mean?"

Zen shifted his bottom and pulled one leg out of the water, crossing it over the other.

"You're going to *hate* Oakville. No big lights or theaters or concerts or restaurants. Just cul-de-sacs and minivans and clones. I'm afraid it's unbelievably dull here."

I scrunched up my face and wondered if all that was true.

Then I said, "You're not dull."

I had never seen such a wide smile or so many teeth. Zen tilted his head and replied, "That is the nicest thing anyone has ever said to me." Then he dropped his shoulders and changed the subject. "May I ask you something, Alice?"

I had no strange allergies or family secrets to hide. "Sure," I said.

"I'm curious. Do you always wear your hair in a ponytail?"

You have to realize that I never thought about the way I looked. My clothes were just there. If it was hot, I wore shorts and a T-shirt. If the temperature dropped, I threw on a sweatshirt. My brown hair was long and stringy, so every day I pulled it back into a ponytail and out of my face. On sunny days, like today, I wore my #8 Red Sox cap.

I replied, "Why do you want to know?"

"You've got to come back to my house," said Zen. Then he stood up and gathered his sneakers with his free hand. "I recently bought a new curling iron, and it crimps too. I did my hair this morning."

I was speechless for two reasons.

First of all, throughout my whole life I had had very

little interest in typical girl stuff like dolls and jewelry and makeup. I preferred video games, and my fave thing in the world (tied with my signed mitt) was the Erector Set. I mean after all, my stay-at-home dad played ball with me and called me Al.

Second of all, some of my best friends had been boys. I always seemed to have more in common with them than I did with girls. But even in the city, I had never met a boy like Zen.

Thankfully (but also unfortunately), my phone rang.

"Must be Pop again," I said and unzipped the outside pocket of my backpack.

Zen whispered, "I'll run ahead and warm up the curling iron."

I watched as he took tiny quick steps back up the swaying dock. He really had to concentrate to keep his balance. I flipped open my phone and read the message: *yaz missing come home*

"Family emergency!" I cried as I grabbed my backpack, slid into my sandals, and whizzed past Zen over the wobbly boards.

He followed me for a few yards, trying to run on bare feet, but soon stopped.

"Oh no!" he cried out. "Anything I can do, Alice?"

My heart pounding, I raced faster than C.Y. himself heading for home plate.

"Keep your eye out for a gray and white tabby cat!" I yelled as I ran the long incline to the stop sign and hung a sharp right down Hemlock Trail.

chapter four

Pop met me in the front yard and tried to explain how Yaz escaped through his legs as he was taking out the trash. I was so out of breath, I could barely understand him. Then he said Mom was next door asking the Lees if they had seen Yaz. I could hear Kissy-Missy yapping up a storm, even though their front door was closed.

It didn't make any sense. Yaz was six years old and had never taken off before. In fact, he had never shown any interest in the outdoors at all until we moved here. It was as if he didn't believe the view from our little apartment in Boston was real. And when we took walks in the city, he stepped carefully down the sidewalk like he was avoiding every piece of trash. But as soon as we arrived in Oakville, Yaz did nothing but sit on the windowsill and meow to go outside. And on our walks he pulled hard on his kitty leash as if he had someplace to go.

I hurried into the house and found Einstein curled up in the corner snoring away, his head cushioned by the chewed-up rubber clown. At first I couldn't tell if he was deeply upset or simply sleeping.

"Einstein, get up!" I nudged him awake and snapped on his collar. He stood slowly and stretched every limb. "I need you to help me look for Yaz!"

As soon as we were outside, Einstein stopped cold.

"No stroller! You have to walk and sniff out Yaz's trail."

But Einstein wouldn't budge, so I gave in. I scurried into the garage and pulled out my old baby stroller. Once in the cushioned seat, Einstein began whimpering. I knew what that meant. I reached behind the stroller pad and pulled out his bonnet.

"There, you big baby—now let's find your brother!"

In the distance I could hear Pop chirping Yaz's name. Mom was now over at the Kings talking to the parents in their driveway. The quadruplet terrors were riding bicycles with training wheels on the lawn circling their house. Suddenly one of them spied me.

"Look! Alice has a stroller!" screamed Juli. All four instantly jumped off their bikes.

Before I knew it, they were chasing Einstein and me around the cul-de-sac. Luckily, they were on foot, so I could outrun them. Einstein loved the race. He planted his paws on the front bar, his bonnet flapping in the wind. All of a sudden he started barking like crazy. I tripped and the bunch of us toppled over each other. The quads and I ended up on the Reeds' lawn as the stroller and Einstein coasted to a stop against the curb.

"Is this your cat, Alice?"

When I looked up Zen was standing in front of us. He held Yaz in one arm, his striped umbrella in the other hand.

"Where did you find him?"

The four girls descended on Zen and pulled at his clothes to get a closer look at my now famous cat. Einstein immediately settled down into the stroller and fell asleep.

"Be gentle!" Zen said firmly. "Kitty's had a very

rough day. In fact, I think he needs a nap. And unless the four of you want naps too, you'd better go home!"

Without a second thought, the quads raced into their yard screeching, then jumped back onto their bikes. I took Yaz from Zen's arm and hugged my cat as tight as a cat allows.

"You charged right past him on the way back from the river," said Zen. "He only got as far as my yard, probably looking for you."

"Thank you so much for finding him."

Mom and Pop appeared and nuzzled Yaz.

"We should give you a reward, young man," said Pop.

"Completely unnecessary," said Zen, "but I would be forever grateful for a glass of lemonade, preferably with ice. I'm practically addicted to the stuff."

"Well, that's a very small reward," replied Mom, "and one we would be happy to offer—I'm sorry, what did you say your name is?"

"Oh, this is Zen," I announced. "The kid I met on my walk."

Pop pulled out leftovers from the week's desserts, and Zen was in heaven. He took a large helping of everything and drank two tall glasses of lemonade. I noticed he crossed his legs like a grown-up when he sat on the stool at the kitchen counter. Einstein licked his orange pants, but Zen didn't like that and shooed him away.

"I'm a cat person," he explained. "I have an aversion to dogs. They're overly affectionate."

"So you and Al are going to be classmates," Pop remarked. "How do you like that? I would have guessed you were older, Zen."

"I am a year older, but I'm glad I stayed back. It's *much* easier."

Pop glanced quickly at Mom.

"But now you'll have to be in school one year longer," I pointed out.

"What are you talking about?" He winced. "As soon as I'm sixteen, I'm quitting that circus and opening a total body salon in California."

"What's a total body salon?" I asked.

Zen leapt off his stool and starting waving his hands

43

around as he spoke. He looked like he was using sign language.

"It's a salon that *celebrates* . . . " He spread his fingers and made big, enthusiastic circles in the air. " . . . the whole person, *inside* . . . " He put a hand over his heart. " . . . and *out*."

Mom and Pop were speechless.

"I refuse to do just hair and nails," Zen continued, tugging at his curls with one hand while wiggling the fingers of the other. "*Or* just yoga and Pilates." Here he kicked one foot out and almost slipped. "I want to shape the total body, even the *spiritual core*." He wrapped his arms around himself and hugged fiercely.

Mom cleared her throat.

"Well, perhaps you'll put that on hold, Zen dear, and go to college first."

"Oooh, I deeply doubt it, Mrs. Bunt," he said, grimacing. "Even my grandmother doesn't think I'm the academic type."

Pop grinned. "That's ridiculous—you're obviously quite bright with big ideas. And you have an excellent vocabulary."

"That's just because I read all day," he said. "I read even more than I drink lemonade."

Mom, the publisher, perked up. "So what do you like? *A Wrinkle in Time*? *Lord of the Flies*? *The Hobbit*?"

"*Celebrity Tips Digest*, *Style Plus*, *Sixteen Magazine*," he replied. "Oh, and I *crave Body by Design*, but it only comes out bi-monthly. They have the best quizzes, like 'What Season Are You?' and 'Is Your Complexion North or South?' That was an amazing one. Turns out, my complexion is definitely north."

I could tell Mom and Pop didn't know how to respond to Zen. They both stared at him, their eyebrows scrunched, mouths dropped open, like they were watching someone sing off-key. I picked up Yaz, who was sound asleep on my lap, and placed him on the floor.

"Want to see my bedroom?" I asked Zen.

He practically choked on a triple-chocolate brownie.

"Oh, I'd love to, Alice!" he cooed. "I'm doing mine over and need some decorating ideas."

He wiped his mouth carefully with a napkin, stood

up, then slid his stool under the counter.

"Thank you for the refreshments, Mr. and Mrs. Bunt."

Mom and Pop continued to stare blankly at Zen, the way I did earlier, when I first met him. And then at the same time they both muttered, "You're welcome."

"Alice," Zen groaned. "Translation, please!" He made a squishy face, all of his features gathering at his nose. "You're actually going to leave it like this?"

"What do you mean *leave it*?" I replied. "I picked it out."

We were upstairs (I still loved saying that) in my bedroom at the end of the hall. There were a few cartons left, but mostly I was unpacked. The walls were chalk white with a baseball theme border. Nine baseball pennants, one for each of my fave baseball teams, were evenly spaced on one wall. A poster of Fenway Park was hanging dead center on another wall under a framed photograph of C.Y. himself. And my bunk beds were against the third wall. I had a desk and matching bureau and even my own bathroom. Oh yeah, and the best part: I had a navy-blue carpet with a picture of a baseball diamond.

"Are you sure the interior decorator knew you were an eleven year-old *girl*?"

Zen's face was still squished in disbelief. I didn't get it. Most boys would have thought this was a great room.

"Do you want to see my autographed mitt?"

"Not particularly," answered Zen.

"My Yokemat cards? My Biker Buddy? My electric drumsticks?"

Zen pretended to faint onto the floor. After a painful moan, he sat up and crossed his thick legs. I was starting to think I had more in common with car-wreck Travis next door.

"Alice, Alice, Alice," he tsk-tsked. Then he tugged on his hair. "You're not a little kid anymore. You're entering middle school."

"So?" I didn't know what he was talking about. Even my pop, who was thirty-nine years old, loved my room.

"Thank the sky above that you met me is all I can say."

"What are you talking about?"

47

Zen glanced down at his watch as if he were on a tight schedule. Then he said, "Meet me at my house first thing tomorrow after church."

"We don't go to church."

"Don't go to church?" Zen stood up awkwardly and pulled at his pants. "Alice Bunt, you don't know what you've been missing!"

chapter five

Pop said most churches end by noon after "the coffee hour," which follows the service. He was on the computer in his office trying to sell a black rotary telephone, the kind my grandparents still had in their summer cabin. Mom was outside digging around, figuring out how to landscape the yard.

"Why, Al?" he asked. He twirled around in his cushy office chair. "Did you want to go to church?"

"I don't know," I said. "I've never been really."

That wasn't entirely true. When I was a toddler, my parents and I attended a Methodist church in the city for about six months. But then Pop decided organized religion was too restrictive. And Mom actually preferred to sleep late on Sundays since she worked such long hours. So we never went again.

"Which one interests you?" he persisted. "A synagogue, a meeting house, a temple, a cathedral, a mosque?"

I covered up his mouth. "Pop, actually I don't want to go to church. Zen told me to stop by *after* church. That's all."

"Oh. Well, he's probably home by now." He returned to typing his Internet ad.

I picked up Yaz, who was meowing at my feet. Einstein scratched at my leg.

"So you don't mind?"

"Mind what, Al?" he mumbled. Then he shook his head and deleted a whole paragraph.

Einstein whimpered and rubbed his face against the back of my knee. I lowered Yaz to the floor, then picked up Einstein.

"Mind if I go to Zen's house?"

Pop retyped the paragraph, then asked, "Why would I mind?"

"I don't know. He's kind of odd."

Yaz looped in and out of my legs. My dad stopped what he was doing and twirled back toward me. He looked down at Yaz and pulled him up into his lap.

"I will admit Zen is a bit different. But he's polite and considerate," said Pop as he stroked Yaz's back. "After all, he found this little guy, didn't he?"

All of that was true, but he wasn't the kid I thought he'd be. I imagined moving to Oakville and finding my very best friend living next door. A kid who loved all my faves, like sports and construction kits and video games and animals. Instead, I was settling for a very strange boy who lived around the corner in a crummy house. More importantly, I didn't want him to crimp my hair or force me to look at magazines.

I wandered upstairs to my room and played a little on my computer, then downstairs to mess around with a video game, then to the basement to build a draw-bridge with my Erector Set . . . but I felt restless. For a little while I watched a dog obedience show on TV and tried to train Einstein to crawl on his belly. But every time I gave the command and tugged his collar, he rolled over onto his back and hiccupped.

I found Yaz sitting on the windowsill, twitching as he

stalked a robin on the front lawn. I stared out the window and down the cul-de-sac at the other three houses, which looked exactly like ours except for their colors. Every family, including us, had a minivan in the driveway. Maybe Zen was right. Maybe we were all dull clones of each other.

Suddenly I wanted to go to his house. I wanted to know why *he* thought I was so lucky to meet him and why I wasn't ready for middle school. This time I didn't bring my backpack, not even a cell phone.

As I slipped on my sandals, Einstein picked up his rubber clown and tottered over to his doggy bed in the kitchen. He was snoring as soon as his head hit the cushion. Yaz, on the other hand, chased my feet, begging to tag along. I had to push him back three times as I squeezed out the front door.

"Make sure Pop doesn't let the cat out," I called over to my mother, who was digging under a tree. She was wearing a pair of overalls that made her look short and wide. "I'm going down the street to Zen's house."

Mom waved her shovel. "Call us when you get

there, dear."

I jogged quickly down the street before the quadruplets noticed me. Just as I banked left in front of the stop sign, I spotted an old lady in Zen's backyard. She was hanging underwear on the clothesline. I assumed this was Zen's grandmother, Babs, so I headed over to introduce myself. I had to climb over a pile of broken clay pots to get close enough to talk.

"Hi, I'm Alice Bunt."

A bunch of clothespins stuck out of her mouth like porcupine quills. After she hung a pair of long purple socks she yanked out all the clothespins at once and snapped, "So what!" Then she stuck the pins back into her mouth and hung a plaid nightgown.

I was startled, then embarrassed.

"I'm here to see Zen," I tried to explain.

She squinted hard at what she was doing like she didn't know what I was talking about.

"Zenithal Stevie Wonder Malinowski?" I inquired.

Finally the old woman finished hanging the wet clothes. She slowly picked up the empty laundry basket. She looked about a hundred years old. Her thin white hair was barely pulled back into a bun. Her lips curled in and her chin stuck out. Her neck was crinkly, like balled-up paper.

Clutching her basket, she limped back to the house without even glancing in my direction and yelled, "Never heard of him!"

"She's mad at me," explained Zen.

As soon as Babs stepped through the back door, Zen appeared from the shed. He was carrying a pile of magazines.

"What is she so mad about?"

Zen shifted the magazines to his other arm and pushed his white-blond curls out of his face.

"We were late for church, because I wanted to crimp my hair with my new curling iron. So she didn't get a vanilla crème-filled donut."

"What?"

Zen climbed the back stairs. He motioned to me to open the door. Immediately, I noticed the strangest smell, like rotten food.

"It's the only way I get her to church every Sunday," he explained. "She *adores* the vanilla crème-filled donuts, but you have to grab one before the Spiritual Chants begin."

"How come?"

"Oh, you can't wait until cocoa hour, because the Food Goddesses buy only a half dozen of the vanilla crème. They're gobbled up before Elder Brightstar even enters the Sacred Space."

What was he talking about?

"Did you say you have 'cocoa hour' at your church?"

We squeezed through the cramped kitchen, which was piled halfway up to the ceiling with pots and books and nearly dead plants.

"Elder Brightstar thinks church should be a celebration of all lives, past and present," said Zen. "So we have a blissful cocoa hour instead of the usual mundane coffee hour."

Elder Brightstar? What kind of church was this?

I followed Zen down the narrow, dark hallway. We

passed Babs. She was now watching an old black-and-white show on the television in a musty family room with shag carpeting. I noticed the whole house still smelled strange: sweet and salty at the same time.

If I thought the kitchen was cluttered, Zen's room was practically stuffed. I hesitated at the doorway. His bedroom was a tiny cube with a single bed in the corner covered with pillows of all shapes and sizes. Plastic crates and boxes, filled with magazines and large seashells, lined the floor. The closet door was partially open with clothes, like a waterfall, pouring out. And the dirty walls were plastered with posters of old-fashioned singers in sequined clothes. Even the windowsill was crammed with candles. The only open space was a small yellow rug in the middle of the room.

"Please come in," said Zen. "I've just started redecorating, so excuse the mess."

I stared at the rug. It was a funny oval shape. "What's that supposed to be?"

Zen dropped the magazines on his bed and replied, "A lemon. Originally it was square, so I cut it, because of course there's no such thing as a square lemon."

I wasn't so sure. In Zen's world anything seemed possible.

He reached under his bed and pulled out a stool and a rectangular mirror the size of a binder. He opened the stand on the back of the mirror and positioned it on the bed. Then he plugged the mirror into the wall and clicked a switch on the cord. Miniature light bulbs lit up all four sides.

"Now sit right here." He pulled the stool in front of the mirror. I felt like he did this every day, like this was his job.

I squatted, my legs scrunched up as if I was sitting on a preschooler's chair. I peered into the mirror. My face was so magnified I could see tiny hairs way up my nose.

Zen clasped his hands and asked, "May I get you anything to drink before we start, Alice? Some lemonade with ice perhaps?"

I stood up instantly and crossed my arms.

"Start what? I don't want to curl or crimp my hair."

"I agree," said Zen. "It has a nice natural wave to it. I'll just go over proper hair care with you and a couple of products you should try."

"Then why do you have that mirror out?"

"So you can take a quiz called 'Who's the Fairest of Them All?' It's in the July/August issue of *Body by Design* and it's very revealing."

"Why would I take a quiz like that?"

Zen smiled and drifted down to the floor, folding his legs.

"Alice, let's talk." He patted the space in front of him.

I wasn't sure I wanted to talk. I couldn't imagine that Zen had anything to say that I needed to hear. He was odd and his room was bizarre and I didn't even understand half his ideas.

I dropped onto the floor anyway and frowned.

"When you're in elementary school," Zen began, gesturing as usual with his hands, "it's fun to play computer games and basketball and whatnot." Then he laughed a little and added, "Of course, *I* never played that stuff, but I know a lot of people who did."

I pushed away from him and leaned back against the bed. I didn't like where this conversation was going.

Zen sat up straight and adjusted his legs. "But now you're older, entering middle school, which is just like pre-high school. It's time to let go of all that elementary stuff and grow up."

This had gone far enough. "My pop still does all that stuff and he's almost forty years old. And Travis, next door to me, plays handheld video games all day *and* he can drive a car."

"Alice," said Zen. "What do your father and Travis have in common that you don't?"

I glanced around the room for clues. I couldn't think of anything that Pop and Travis had in common.

"Give up?" asked Zen. Then he answered his own question. "They're both boys. You are not."

I tried so hard not to say what came out of my mouth, but Zen wasn't being fair.

"You're a boy too, but *you* don't act like one."

The next thing I knew, Zen's face turned completely red, as if no one had ever told him that before. He jumped up, which was a struggle, and placed his hands on his hips.

"I was trying to help by getting you ready for Sachem Regional Middle School, because believe me, you're not the least bit ready. And it starts in only two weeks! I gathered all my premium magazines and had your skin tone picked out and everything. But if you're going to be mean, then you can forget it!"

Just then the phone rang. Out in the family room, Babs answered after the first ring. "Never heard of Alice Bunt!" she yelled and slammed the phone down.

"Oh no, my mother!" I said, standing up. "I forgot to call."

Zen ignored me and scooped up the magazines from the bed. I felt badly that he was so upset, but I didn't need tips on how to be a girl, particularly from a strange boy like Zen.

"I guess you better go home," he said. He folded the mirror, placed it on the stool, and shoved them both under the bed.

I tried to end on a good note. "Thanks for having me

over," I said. "I like your—" I searched the room for something to compliment. "I like your lemon rug."

Then I took off as fast I could.

Chapter Six

A week passed.

I did spot Zen a couple of times. Once when we drove by, he was sitting on the lounge chair in his shady front yard, sipping lemonade through a straw and reading a magazine. Another time, I saw him helping Babs out to the Volkswagen Bug. I couldn't imagine her driving a car.

I can't say I thought about Zen too much or even felt badly about our spat. Not really. After all, what did he know about being a girl? Even though he liked the usual girlie junk, like movie stars and magazines and curling irons, none of that made him a girl. It was the same with me. I knew some people thought I was a tomboy, because I liked typical boy things like baseball and video games and building stuff. But that didn't make me a boy.

The week flew by anyway, because I was busy with Pop having a blast. One afternoon we drove to Portland, Maine, to see a Sea Dogs minor league baseball game. Another day, my friend Marky Dukakis drove up from the city with his father, and they spent the night. Two times, Pop and I fished for stripers from the ocean shore. And best of all, the Kings and their quadruplet terrors were away camping in New Hampshire while their floors were being sanded.

But something about this new life wasn't so great. Other than Zen, I still hadn't met anyone around my age in Oakville. And middle school was starting in one week! I was feeling pretty anxious. What if Zen was a little bit right? What if I wasn't ready for Sachem Regional?

And then Yaz disappeared. *Again.*

Pop and I had just carried my bounce-back pitching net from the garage to the backyard. All excited, I ran into the house to grab my fave C.Y. baseball mitt. Within a millisecond, as I opened the back door, Yaz squeezed through and took off around our house toward the cul-de-sac, like he was chasing a chocolate-covered mouse. I raced after him as fast as I could, only to catch sight of his tail as it disappeared around the bend in the road.

I dashed back into the house and dialed Zen's number. Thankfully, he (and not Babs) answered the phone.

In one big breath, I said, "Zen-it's-Alice-Yaz-took-off-again-can-you-*please*-run-outside-and-try-to-catch-him?"

Before he could answer I hung up and ran across the yard and down the street. Pop stood in the middle of the cul-de-sac, shaking his head.

"Come right back, Al, if you can't find him!"

But I did find Yaz, or, I should say, Zen did. Together they were sitting in Zen's front yard in the ratty lounge chair under the old tree. Yaz was blissfully curled up in Zen's lap and licking his hand, as if they had been there for hours. I was the only one completely upset and out of breath.

"I can't believe he ran away *again*," I practically

hollered. "He's never done anything like this before."

Zen glanced up, smiling, stroking Yaz's back. He shrugged his shoulders and said, "Kitty obviously dislikes living on Hemlock*less* Trail."

I frowned and pulled Yaz carefully into my arms.

"I'll make sure he stays in the house from now on."

"Oh Alice, he can come over anytime," Zen replied. "I truly adore felines. Unfortunately, Babs is allergic, a sinus thing. So I have to wait until I open my total body salon and get my own apartment before I can have one."

As usual, Zen was telling me way more than I wanted to know. To keep him from rambling, I gave a quick *see ya* wave and headed toward the street.

"Oh, Alice?"

Just past the stop sign I turned around and took a deep breath.

"Yes?"

"Figured out your BTS outfit yet?" he asked.

"What? I can't hear you."

I had to cling to Yaz, who was restlessly clawing at my arms.

From alice to zen

Zen stood up and pulled a piece of paper from his back pocket. He was wearing cut-offs again, but today they were long with fringe hanging past his knees. His T-shirt was pale green with a giant peace sign and he wore a straw hat over his curls.

He hurried toward me as he pointed to the ripped-out magazine page. "I saw this in the *Fashion Forward* fall issue this morning before church. Right away I knew this had to be your BTS outfit."

I could tell he was hesitating a little, like he knew it was peculiar to choose somebody else's wardrobe. I didn't know what to say. I didn't want to hurt his feelings again so I asked, "What's a BTS outfit?"

"*Back-To-School* clothes," he replied, grinning. "You know that first day of school will be absolutely HUGE for you, because it's middle school *and* you're the new kid."

Now I was feeling very anxious.

"What do you mean by HUGE?"

Zen stepped back and crossed his arms. "I mean it could decide your status, where you'll fit, which clique will claim you!"

"Just by the clothes I wear on the first day?"

He nodded, adding, "It's by far the most important day of your life."

At that moment, Yaz managed to wriggle out of my arms and slither between Zen's feet. He scooped him up and they nuzzled.

"Wow, he really likes you."

"That's because I'm so much of a feline myself. I have hundreds of catlike qualities. I'm convinced I was a cat in a past life."

To be honest, Zen reminded me a lot more of Einstein than Yaz, but I kept my mouth shut.

"Oh, Alice, I have a fantastic idea!" exclaimed Zen as he handed Yaz back to me. "Let me walk you home and help you control Kitty so he doesn't run away again. Then I can peek in your closet and try to pull a BTS outfit together for you like the one in this photo."

I searched for an excuse. Previous plans? Relatives visiting? Not feeling well? And then I decided it wouldn't hurt to have him help me with my wardrobe. Truthfully, I kind of liked the outfit in the picture. But more importantly, I really wanted to fit in at school.

"Sure, why not."

So together we wandered back up Hemlock Trail. Me—small, precise Alice Bunt (with cat)—alongside big, boisterous Zenithal Stevie Wonder Malinowski (with umbrella). There could not have been two more opposite sixth-graders in all of Oakville.

I swear, within thirty minutes every single piece of clothing I owned was spread out somewhere in my bedroom. Zen would hold up an item like a shirt, turn it around, sigh, then toss it to one side or the other. I waited, reclined across my bed facedown with Einstein slumbering across the back of my knees. Yaz followed Zen's feet as if assisting in the fashion decisions.

"Okay!" Zen finally announced. "I want to see this tank top with these jeans. You'll need your mother to drive you to the mall to get a wide tan belt decorated with some kind of jewels or even silver studs. Suzannah's or the Clothes Bug should have it. Oh, and find a choker with teeny pearls, something really delicate.

I forgot to look, do you have pierced ears?"

I was too stunned to answer.

"No? Too bad. And shoes? I would buy some kind of toeless suede slip-on, but if you have to, you can wear these little green sneakers, but no socks. And wash the laces, they're filthy."

I slid Einstein off my legs and onto the bed. Slowly I sat up and asked, "What?"

"What *what*?" replied Zen.

"What did you just say? How am I supposed to remember all that?"

Zen scurried over to my desk. "Not to worry," he said, "I'll write it all down."

I felt so confused. Not only did I have no idea where the mall was, but I hated the mall, any mall. And my mother never took me shopping. Pop bought all my clothes online.

I stared at the list and reluctantly promised Zen that I would call him *if and when* I returned from the dreaded mall.

Chapter Seven

To my surprise, my mother was thrilled to drive me to the mall—and she knew exactly where it was. In fact, she had already been there twice to buy throw pillows for the couch and a new set of mixing bowls for Pop. She even took the morning off from work. We arrived early Monday, the moment the stores opened.

The name of the mall was Deer Run Square, which was a pretty ridiculous name since, obviously, there were no more deer running around the square. It was just what Zen had said about Hemlock Trail. They had to cut down all the trees to make the trail. I knew the builders chose names that would make the neighborhood sound nicer, but ever since Zen pointed that out, the phony names were starting to bother me too.

As soon as we arrived at Deer Run Square, my

mother pulled a mall map from her pocketbook.

"Where shall we go first?" she asked, spreading the map across my lap. "Eames Department Store is at this end, and on the north side is The Closet Company." She pointed to each place.

I pulled Zen's list from my pocket.

"I'm supposed to go to either Suzannah's or the Clothes Bug for the belt."

"But don't you want to shop at a few other places, dear? We could buy you some school outfits or a purse or a pretty nightgown or perhaps some lip gloss?"

I was beginning to think that my mother should have brought Zen instead of me. I never realized how much she enjoyed shopping for this junk. Most of my free time was spent with Pop, and it had never occurred to either of us to go to the mall and buy lip gloss.

I replied, "Not really."

Mom looked disappointed, but only for a second. I guess she knew she had to take what she could get.

"Okay. We'll try Suzannah's *and* the Clothes Bug, just to compare. Then if you're up for it, dear, we'll buy some hot pretzels."

The mall seemed packed for a Monday morning, but my mother said the mall was always packed. We located Suzannah's on the map and headed to the second floor on the escalator. A few people were gathered by a fountain where a lady was playing a violin. Mom wanted to stop and listen, but I tugged her in the direction of the store. I wanted to get this over with and back home. Pop and I were building a go-kart out in the garage with a real engine from our old lawn mower.

The second we walked into Suzannah's I knew why Zen had recommended it. It was full of his fave stuff like hair accessories and lots and lots of frilly items.

Mom tried not to look excited, but I could tell she wanted me to try on everything. I, on the other hand, started to sweat a little. This place was like a foreign country. Maybe someday it would all interest me. But at that moment I just wanted to be under the go-kart, my hands covered in lube oil.

My mother asked a saleslady where the belts were. She led us to the corner of the store where a long rack was covered in gobs of belts of all lengths and colors.

"Your daughter's very petite," said the sales lady, as if I wasn't standing right there. "I doubt we have anything *that* little."

I immediately reasoned that even if I did want to fit in at middle school, I was too tiny for the uniform.

"Pop and I could always cut a few extra holes," I suggested.

"Let's try the Clothes Bug," whispered Mom. "They may have smaller sizes, dear."

But like Suzannah's, the Clothes Bug only carried junior and adult, while I still wore a girls' 10-12. I would probably be the only student in the entire middle school still wearing little-kid sizes. Suddenly, from the clearance rack my mother let out a mini shriek.

"Alice, I found a double-zero that might work!"

The belt was almost perfect, tan and wide with swirly cutout designs. They weren't jewels, but they'd have to do. I was so relieved that I was willing to look at the necklaces. Right away, I found a choker with itty-bitty colorful beads, close to what Zen had instructed.

"How about a tube of peach lip gloss?" my mother asked. "It's only a dollar."

I gave in, making my mother's trip to the mall almost complete. On the way out we bought a bag of hot pretzels and sat down to eat on a bench near the lady playing the violin.

"See? This *was* fun," said Mom. "Maybe we can do it more often."

This definitely wasn't my idea of fun, but I was really glad to spend a Monday morning with my mother. And I was totally relieved to find the right stuff for school. I shrugged my shoulders and replied, "Yeah, maybe."

"I'll be over in two shakes, Alice. I just got back from Sacred Songsters rehearsal and it was a real humdinger. Elder Brightstar practically fainted after "Earth and Air, Everywhere." We were super harmonious!"

I had no idea what Zen was babbling about, but I was pretty excited about my BTS outfit. It looked almost identical to the one in the magazine. Even Pop said I could have been the model in the picture.

While I waited for Zen by the dining room window in my new clothes, I examined myself in the large formal mirror. Zen had chosen a striped tank top, a gift from my aunt in Minnesota, which I had never worn. Then he found some faded jeans and rolled up each pant leg to my knees. I wore my green sneakers and the new tan belt. And the necklace kind of pulled it all together with multicolored beads. It was as if Zen knew exactly what I would wear if I ever really thought about it. He was pretty good at this total body salon stuff.

All of a sudden, Yaz started racing in circles. I peered out the window. Over the horizon, I spotted Zen rushing up Hemlock Trail, one hand swinging at his side, the other carrying the *BODY BY DESIGN* umbrella. He was smiling wide, like always, as if he were hiding a surprise. That made me smile. I threw open the door.

"There's my little *Gladys*!" he said as he lifted Yaz to his face.

"What did you just call my cat?" I asked, confused as usual by the direction of our conversation. Not to be left out, Einstein wedged his square frame in between my feet.

"Gladys! After one of the greatest Motown legends of all time—along with her backup singers, the Pips, of course. That's what I would have named Kitty, Gladys Knight. But I know he's named after some basketball player or whatever."

"*Base*ball!" I corrected him. "He's named after my fave baseball player of all time. And Yaz is definitely a *he*. Gladys sounds like a girl's name."

"Of course it does, but animals don't really care what you call them, Alice."

I couldn't keep up with Zen's illogical logic. He was as unpredictable as the direction of the wind. It was like he took everything I knew and blew it upside down and inside out.

Zen suddenly gushed, "Don't tell me, is this your BTS outfit?"

I had almost forgotten about my new clothes. "Yep, my mom took me to the mall and we got this belt and necklace."

Still stroking Yaz, Zen said, "Move into the light and

turn."

I stepped over Einstein and into a patch of sun. Sticking my arms straight out, I spun slowly.

"Turn the other way."

"*Zen*," I complained.

"Just once," he insisted. "I need to see every angle."

I couldn't tell what he was thinking and started to wonder if I should have asked Mom for the toeless suede slip-ons.

"You're gorgeous!" he announced. "Now all we have to work on is your coif, your cosmetics, your academic sundries, your clique, and, of course, your promenade."

"My promo-what?"

"The way you walk!"

I was so thrilled by Zen's initial "gorgeous" compliment that I didn't exactly register everything he said. In fact, I hadn't understood a word of what he said, except the last part about my walk. But what did the way I walk have to do with anything?

Zen yelled, "Sachem Regional Middle School, make way for Miss Alice Bunt!"

chapter eight

It had never occurred to me, back in the city, that I wasn't ready for middle school. If I were still living in my old neighborhood, I wouldn't have thought once about my BTS outfit until an hour before school started. Since it was always hot on the first day, I would have worn shorts and sandals. I might have brushed my teeth an extra minute or so and tried to find a colorful elastic for my ponytail, but that would have been it. Pop would serve rocket waffles, since it was a special day. Then Mom would walk Marky Dukakis and me to school on her way to the subway.

But here I was in the suburbs, spending the last precious days of summer molding me, Alice Bunt, into a sixth-grade girl. Because according to Zenithal Stevie Wonder Malinowski and his magazines, I knew next to nothing about preteen culture.

The following day, Tuesday, we worked on "my coif" (translation: my hair) over at Zen's house. He knew I didn't want it crimped or anything girlie. Instead, I let him trim my split-ends, then spray my hair with gel. Next he told me to hold my head upside-down and shake as he blow-dried. Zen claimed he had read all about "quick and easy long-hair care" in *Celebrity Tips Digest*.

"I can't believe you've been hiding this in a ponytail," he remarked. "Promise me, Alice, you'll wear your hair loose from now on. It's pure silk."

As he worked on my new look, I glanced around Zen's bedroom. I noticed everything was a bit more organized than before. His clothes were hanging in the closet, and a few plastic crates were missing. The colorful bedspread was new too. I asked Zen about the lines of candles around the room.

"I collect them, but only sacred herbal scents like lavender or sage. I won't buy those fake smelly kinds."

I didn't ask why. I was starting to learn that there was

no explaining Zen. The more I knew him the less I understood.

"Who are all these people in these posters?" I asked pointing toward the walls. In every picture the performers smiled as wide as Zen did. But their teeth were as bright as their sparkly outfits.

"Don't tell me you don't recognize only the best Motown singers in the history of popular music?" he asked, truly surprised. He even stopped working on my hair for a moment.

"That's the queen, Diana Ross, and her Supremes. Those are the Four Tops and that group is The Temptations. Over there is Smokey Robinson and the Miracles. And of course that's the one and only—other than me—Stevie Wonder. I'll have to play you a Motown recording, Alice, but not yet. You're not quite ready."

The following morning back at my house, Zen insisted I try applying "cosmetics" (translation: makeup). He said I couldn't hate it until I'd experienced it at least once. Then he was shocked to hear that I didn't own any makeup, other than the lip gloss I had bought at the mall. So I searched through my mother's drawers and found enough variety to satisfy even him.

"Oh no! We have a major problem, Alice," Zen said, making his squishy face. He held open a page of *La Mode Magazine*. "Look at this color chart. Your eyelids scream for pale pinks and earth tones." He sighed loudly as he studied my mother's eye shadow case. "All I have here are blues and purples."

"You know," I explained as nicely as possible, "even if I wanted to wear makeup, Mom and Pop would never allow me to wear it to school. Maybe to a party or something, but that would be it."

"Oh, that's not good." Zen scooted in a bit too close and studied my face. "Okay, here's what we'll do—a dash of blush, some brown mascara, your lip gloss, and a touch of clear powder. I promise it will look totally natural. You won't hate it and your parents won't even know it's there."

I hesitated, then finally agreed. After all, we were just trying it out, and Zen seemed to know what he was doing. And in the end I decided makeup wasn't so bad. It was just a little itchy.

On Thursday, Pop took us to Chain-Mart. He waited in the minivan as Zen and I shopped for "academic sundries" (translation: school supplies). Pop gave us each twenty-five dollars to buy everything we needed. Zen offered to vacuum our whole house for the money, but Pop refused—unless down the road Zen dropped out of high school. Then, he joked, Zen would owe him the interest as well.

At Chain-Mart, as instructed by Zen's *Tween Magazine*, each of us picked a favorite theme and went with it. For example, I liked navy blue and baseball. So I chose a dark blue binder, folders featuring the Red Sox, and pencils in the shape of bats. Zen convinced me to exchange the bats for regular pencils and to add a different color to the mix. So I chose a red assignment notebook and a set of black ballpoint pens.

Zen, on the other hand, picked out a yellow polka-dot binder and metallic folders. He said his theme was based on the "psychedelic era" of the late 1960s, whatever that meant. His pens were neon and his assignment notebook lime green. I thought it was peculiar for a boy to pick out the shiniest items in the store. But so far, Zen seemed to know exactly what middle-school kids liked. After all, he was the one always studying the latest fashions in those magazines, not me.

A day later, as I was brushing the annoying tangles out of my "silky" long hair, Zen called and suggested we meet down at the river. He said he had something that would make me possibly one of the most popular girls in the entire sixth grade.

I rushed down the stairs and grabbed my sandals from the front closet. Yaz was going crazy as I scurried around, and even Einstein whimpered a little at my feet. Lately, I had been neglecting my pets and also Pop—we weren't even a quarter of the way done building the go-kart. But not counting today, I had only two days left until middle school started. And it seemed like the more I did to get ready for Sachem Regional, the more Zen wanted me to do!

He was waiting for me at the end of Old Man

Weagan's dock. Even though the sky was cloudy, Zen shaded himself with his striped umbrella. In his other hand, he held a thick book and, of course, a magazine.

"Here it is, Alice," he said, twisting around as his pale feet dangled in the water. "My elementary school yearbook!"

I was confused. How was that supposed to make me instantly popular? As I slipped off my sandals, Zen explained the fantastic idea he had come up with in the middle of the night. With his yearbook, Zen announced, he would find my "social clique" (translation: my group of friends). But only after I filled out a quick questionnaire from *Sixteen Magazine*.

"I just turned eleven in April," I pointed out. "I don't want to look *sixteen* yet."

"This quiz has nothing to do with age, Alice," he said. "It would help a five-year-old make friends in kindergarten, I swear."

I sat down and held Zen's umbrella as he found the right page in the magazine. He pulled a new neon pen from his back pocket.

"Now answer these twelve easy questions," he instructed. "Take all the time you need."

I handed the umbrella back and glanced over the quiz. It was entitled "Loner or Leader, Which One Are You?" It asked really strange questions, like which kind of bread I preferred and if I slept on my stomach or my back.

After I finished, Zen said, "According to the scoring chart you're a heart/tree with a total of 17."

"Huh?"

Zen wriggled around and sat up straighter, as if the results of the quiz were absolutely critical to my social success.

"The heart means you're nice, because you get upset when you hurt someone else's feelings. And the tree means you're a loyal friend and despise gossip."

"Well, what does the 17 mean?"

Zen ran his finger along the graph and explained, "The 17 is where you fit on the Loner or Leader scale of 1 to 20." Then he gushed, "Oh Alice, that's better than I expected! You're a 17, much closer to a leader than a loner!"

"I am?" I peered at the magazine. "It can tell all that about me from those twelve questions?"

"Oh, I think it describes you precisely," said Zen. He smiled proudly, as if he were personally responsible for my high score.

I had never thought of myself as either a leader or a loner. In fact, until that quiz, I had never thought of those things at all.

"Okay," said Zen, shifting his legs as he opened up his elementary school yearbook. "Going by your fantastic score of 17, let's find your *clique*."

He laughed nervously, like we were opening the pages of a stolen diary.

"It's alphabetical by last name, so we'll start with Rebecca Aulowitz," he began, pointing to a small photo of a girl with glasses. "She's a capital N-O!"

I pulled back and frowned. "What do you mean? What's wrong with her?"

"Totally unpopular, shy, poor dresser, thin hair, probably a 3 at best."

And that's what Zen did for the next hour. He read

off each name and determined their step on the "Loner or Leader" ladder. For me, he chose girls close to the top of preteen royalty. Specifically, I was to befriend Haley Benson and Yvette Mimmick (definitely 17s like me).

As Zen pointed and babbled and flipped through the pages of his yearbook, my stomach began to cramp. Back in the city, I had been excited about moving to a new school and meeting new kids. In the past, I had always made friends easily, but I had never considered their popularity index. If I liked them and they liked me, then we were friends. But listening to Zen, I felt like I was auditioning for a Hollywood movie. The only problem was I didn't know which character I wanted to play or if I even wanted a part.

chapter nine

On Saturday, just two days before the first day of school, Zen had one last thing to talk about: the way I walked. I had no idea what he was going to say, but I figured it couldn't take more than a few minutes.

Was I ever wrong.

We were sitting on the lemon rug in his room, leaning against his bed. Somehow Zen had cleared out even more stuff and I could actually see the floor. A new collection made up of colorful shells was arranged on a glass shelf above his bed.

"Did you paint those seashells?" I asked.

Zen was skimming through a magazine and putting sticky notes on various pages.

"The shells?" he repeated, looking up from his reading. "Oh yes. I paint them according to my mood, like blue if I'm sad or red if I'm angry or green if I feel envious. Then I inscribe a tiny message inside expressing my mood, like 'You insulted me, Babs.' Stuff like that. It's very therapeutic."

Zen returned to reading his magazine, and I studied the shells. Most of them were either blue or red with a few greens. I spotted a yellow one on the end and wondered if it was a "happy" shell.

Suddenly, Zen stood up and balanced a book on his pile of white-blond curls. He told me to grab a book too. I stood up across from him and placed it on my head.

"You know, Alice," he began, frozen in concentration, "if I could teach a class on how to walk, the world would be a far more joyful place."

At first, I had no idea what that meant. Did he mean people who couldn't walk, like people in wheelchairs? And if he thought he could teach everyone how to walk, why did he himself always walk in such a hurry?

"Look forward, Alice, chin up, shoulders back."

Even as I did what Zen told me to do, I noticed he wasn't doing it correctly. He jutted his jaw way out and let his round stomach roll forward. He even licked his lips like it helped him to focus.

"I read all about good posture in *Body by Design*," said Zen, who was now talking very slowly because he was straining to hold his position. "It can make all the difference in your life, from the way your clothes fit to increasing longevity."

Standing with the book on my head was so easy I started racing around the room. I even gave a little hop right in front of Zen, which broke his concentration, causing his book to slip off his crinkled curls. He quickly moved on to the next lesson.

"Let's loosen up!" Zen picked up the magazine from the floor. "On page ninety-four they have five excellent tips on warming up before you walk."

"Don't you walk to warm up?" I asked. "Why would you warm up before you walk?"

He pointed at *Body by Design* and said, "Walking correctly, which means warming up first, improves our health, our confidence and our energy. It's all here on page ninety-four."

Zen spread his legs and placed his arms at his side. Next he started to do something like a mixed-up jumping jack, with his arms opening when they should have been closing.

"Let's see at least ten of these, Alice!" he said too loudly, as he could barely talk and breathe at the same time.

And so we went through five exercises, ten times each. They were simple and easy and most likely meant for senior citizens. By the time we were finished, he was very red and had to sit down.

After catching his breath, Zen pulled a crate of old record albums out of his closet. He flipped through them until he found what he was looking for.

"Here's one of my favorite Motown groups," he said, holding up an album. "Martha and the Vandellas."

The cover photo was the same picture as one of the posters on the wall. The three ladies were dressed in blue gowns and posing perfectly, like store mannequins.

"You have a real record player?" I asked.

"It's Babs's."

"You should let my pop know if she ever wants to sell it. He could probably get her a lot of money for it on the Internet."

Zen grabbed his throat. "We would never sell it! How else would I listen to my Motown music?"

"On an MP3 or even a CD?" I suggested.

"Um, hello? I don't own every little modern gadget?"

I didn't tell him he could buy one with the money they could get for the record player. For some reason, those Motown albums seemed particularly special to Zen.

We moved out into the family room, where Babs was watching one of those old television shows in black and white. A freckled boy was sitting on his television father's lap and calling him Pa.

"Babs, Alice and I need some privacy. Do you mind?"

She snapped back in her raspy voice. "Put a lid on it!"

"But I need to play some Motown tunes!"

"Listen!" she croaked. "Sheriff Andy's about to punish Opie and Aunt Bee doesn't think he should, but I hope he does it!"

"You've seen that *Andy Griffith* episode at least twenty-nine times," said Zen irritably. "Andy tells Aunt Bee to mind her own business, and she stops talking to him. Then they all make up and eat pie."

"*Hazelnuts!*" She waved her hand at Zen. "You ruined the ending again!"

She stood up, shut the television off with her foot, and grumbled as she limped out of the room. A few seconds later a door slammed.

I had never met a family who constantly barked at each other. The two of them reminded me of the scrappy mutts you see at the pound. For a second, I didn't blame Zen's mother for leaving and never coming back.

"Now let's learn how to *really* walk!" said Zen.

He placed the needle carefully onto the spinning record album.

"Pay attention to the Vandellas' unique style," he added, as the ladies' voices popped out of the old record player like a jack-in-the-box.

Zen turned and strutted across the floor as a celebrity does on the red carpet. The only problem was the room was terribly crowded. He could barely take three steps before he had to turn around and strut the other way. He groaned and lifted the needle off the record.

"Can we do this at your house, Alice? Your rec room would be ideal."

"But we don't own a record player."

"Not a problem— I'll carry this one over."

Ten minutes later we were set up in the basement of my house. Yaz was thrilled to see Zen, and Einstein was happy for anyone's company. We played with them for a few minutes until Zen insisted we get to work.

"When you promenade," he explained, "you should hear specific music in your head. That way, you're centered on the actual walking."

"Huh?" I asked.

"I'll use myself as an example." Zen scurried over to the record player. I figured he wasn't doing his real walking yet.

"When I walk, I *always* hear Motown music playing in my mind. Watch me, Alice."

Zen placed the needle down on the record once again, then stood at attention. As the music began, he rolled his head around a bit as we did in exercise number three from page ninety-four of the magazine.

Suddenly, Martha and the Vandellas burst into a song about a new kind of music, a new rhythm for the whole wide world to celebrate.

And Zen walked. Actually, it was more like a march, as if he were in a parade about to wave at everyone. He was practically kicking his legs in the air.

"Promenade with me, Alice!" he ordered.

So I did.

I followed Zen up and down the long rec room to the bouncy beat of Motown. And pretty soon, Einstein was trotting behind us as Yaz zigzagged across the floor.

Then out of the blue, Zen broke out singing—and I stopped in my tracks. I couldn't believe it. His voice was the best I had heard in my entire life. It was better than Martha and both of the Vandellas put together.

By the end of the song, Zen was completely out of breath. He rushed over to turn off the record player.

"You're getting it, Alice," he said, panting. "Now don't be discouraged. It just takes confidence."

He turned around and saw me still staring.

"What's the matter?"

"Wow!" I said. "I didn't know you could sing like that."

In fact, up until that point, I didn't know Zen could do anything other than follow the advice of magazines.

"Oh, that," he replied. "If you think I'm good, you should hear Wintermoon over at our church."

Did he say Wintermoon?

Zen sighed. "He gets most of the solos."

"Well, I bet you'll be getting most of the solos soon," I said, and I meant it.

Just then Zen cried, "Alice, I have a fantastic idea! Why don't you come to church with Babs and me tomorrow morning? You can wear your BTS outfit and do your hair and makeup and practice your walk. It will be a trial run before school on Monday."

I didn't know what to say. Back in the city, most people I knew went to either a Protestant or Catholic church. Some of my friends were Jewish, and there was a Muslim family on our street. In the back of my mind I had this vague idea that churches and temples were usually quiet and full of people praying. But Zen's church sounded different, *really* different.

"What kind of church is it anyway?" I asked.

"The Seacoast Spiritual Center," Zen grinned. "Sacred home of the most harmonious chanting and singing on the pure green earth!"

Chapter ten

Mom and Pop thought it was a good idea for me to go to Zen's church. They said that it was important I was exposed to beliefs different from their own. I have to admit I was a little curious about Zen's church, but more importantly, I wanted to see how long it would take to get my whole BTS look together.

My hair was pretty quick and easy, but the makeup looked horrible. I brushed on too much mascara, so dots appeared above my eyes. And one cheek had way more blush than the other. The time it took to straighten out my face was longer than it took to do my hair. Finally, I slipped into my BTS outfit and stared at myself in the full-length mirror. It was strange. I looked pretty good, but I didn't feel like me.

As I turned to walk out of the bathroom, I tried to remember one of the songs from Zen's record album. But all I could think of was "Take Me Out to the Ball Game," which made me walk kind of funny.

Mom and Pop were still lounging in bed like they always did on Sunday mornings. I poked my head in to let them know I was leaving.

"Don't you look snazzy, Al!" Pop exclaimed.

"Lovely!" added Mom. "Do you have your cell phone, dear?"

"And your safety whistle?" added Pop.

"Right here," I said, patting my pocket.

Then Mom peered further over her newspaper and said, "You look slightly flushed, dear. Are you feeling okay?"

"Yep." I wiped some of the makeup from my cheeks. "I'll be back by lunch."

Zen and his grandmother were waiting for me in front of their house. Actually, Babs was already in the car in the driver's seat. All of a sudden, I wondered if she could really drive.

"Alice Bunt, you look amazing! Exactly like the popular girls at school," Zen said.

He took me by the shoulders and turned me around.

From alice to zen

I think I felt myself blush, which made my powdered cheeks even itchier.

Wearing dark pants and a blue dress shirt, Zen actually looked nice in a normal outfit. And his hair was slightly wavy, not crimped, and parted to the side.

"So do you," I said. "I mean, you look good for a boy."

He grabbed the collar of his shirt. "Isn't this hideous?" he moaned. "I have to wear it for Sacred Songs Circle. It's the only time you'll ever see me conform."

Just then, Babs blasted the horn so loudly my heart skipped a beat. She rolled down the window and yelled, "Get a move on it! I want to grab a donut before that cockamamie service starts."

We climbed into the back seat of the Volkswagen Bug, which was filthy. The upholstery was ripped and a spring in the seat was poking out. The car was the old kind of Bug, with a seatbelt that crossed your waist only, no shoulder strap. I pulled the belt as tight over my lap as I could.

All the way to church, Zen hummed up and down the scale, claiming he had to exercise his vocal chords before singing. It was a good thing he didn't want to talk, because Babs's driving made me sick to my stomach. Her seat was pushed up against the steering wheel so that her face was inches from the windshield. And she drove in fast, jerky motions, the same way she talked.

As Babs skidded into the parking lot, Zen exclaimed, "Looks like a full Sacred Circle today!" There had to have been at least thirty cars already parked.

"They better have some of those vanilla crème-filled donuts left!" yelled Babs.

The huge round sign at the entrance read:

SEACOAST SPIRITUAL CENTER
hosted by Elder Brightstar
"I have the right to respect what I am."

That didn't sound very religious to me—but I decided not to ask.

The church did not look anything at all like a church from the outside. More like a dairy barn. It was a bright red building with tiny windows. A huge rainbow was painted across the roof above the word *Blessings*.

Babs raced ahead of us.

"Let her get her donuts," said Zen. "I don't want to sit with her anyway."

As we entered the red barn church everyone greeted Zen. But they said, "Good Tidings, Brother Zenithal," like we were pilgrims. People of all colors and ages and abilities (and some wearing even more peculiar outfits than Zen usually wore) came over to give him a hug or shake his hand. I had never seen such a variety of people in one place. And all with such unusual names like Motherheart and Summerland.

I glanced around and spied Babs behind a table in the corner, stuffing a donut in her mouth.

When a woman up front began playing her harp, everyone rushed to sit down. I thought all churches had rows of pews like benches, but we sat in folding metal chairs in one giant circle. A white flower had been placed on each seat. Like everyone else, I picked up mine and held it in my lap.

Elder Brightstar strolled out from a side door wearing a light blue robe. A garland of ivy (I think it was plastic) was draped around his head. He walked to the center of our circle of chairs, closed his eyes and began chanting: "Hear the voice that sings in you, it creates the world anew."

From then on the whole congregation chanted and clapped and chanted and twirled and chanted and stomped. Sometimes Elder Brightstar yelled at the ceiling in a loud, god-like voice, and other times he stared in silence for what seemed like an hour. I couldn't follow a thing that was going on, but I could tell that Zen was having a wonderful time.

Near the end of the service, Zen and about two dozen others (all wearing dark pants or skirts and blue shirts) stood and walked outside the circle. Elder Brightstar handed them choir robes tie-dyed in wild colors, just like a T-shirt I had made at camp one summer. The group stretched their arms and held hands, encircling our circle of chairs. (It reminded me a little of duck-duck-goose.)

"Brother Zenithal!" Elder Brightstar called out. "As the youngest member of our Sacred Songsters, will you please joyfully lead us in 'Earth and Air, Everywhere!' "

The Sacred Songsters immediately began swaying back and forth, followed by the rest of us, still sitting in the folding metal chairs. Except Elder Brightstar. He closed his eyes and smiled like he was thinking about those donuts. After the harpist played a few measures, Zen belted out the first notes of "Earth and Air, Everywhere!" just as loudly as a Motown superstar. I was so happy he had a solo.

After the singing was done and the service was over, everyone turned to hug one another and say something that sounded like "Brightest Blessings." A very heavy woman wearing a flowery dress and a purple hat turned to me and gave me a squeeze. She smelled like Chinese take-out.

"What did you think of that, Alice?" Zen was standing in front of me, bright red, breathing hard. "Is the world refreshed or *what*?"

I didn't know what to say. I was still shocked by my first visit to church. It wasn't at all what I had expected.

"You sang even better than you did yesterday in my

basement. And you had a solo!"

Zen smiled ear to ear. "Well you should come when Wintermoon is here. His voice will purify your spirit."

During cocoa hour, everyone complimented Zen. It was like he was one of those celebrities in his magazines. As we left the red barn church and headed across the parking lot, I noticed his head was high and his shoulders were back. He was definitely walking to the music in his head.

When we arrived at the car, I was surprised to find Babs already sitting in the driver's seat, the engine running. On her cheek was a dab of vanilla crème filling.

"Get a move on it," she snapped, "before those crazies start begging us for cash!"

We returned to the little green ranch house exactly at noon. Babs charged into the driveway, then slammed on the brakes before she bumped the shed. As soon as she turned off the ignition, she threw open the car door and limped as quickly as she could across the yard.

"*Andy Griffith* comes on again at twelve o'clock," explained Zen. We climbed out of the backseat. "She can't stand to miss an episode."

"Do you want to come over to my house for lunch?" I asked. "I think Pop is making homemade pizza. He usually does on Sundays."

Zen said he was tempted, but he had tons to do before school the next day, like finalizing his BTS outfit and organizing his backpack. Then he told me to make sure I stopped by his house before the bus arrived in the morning.

"I can't. My mom's driving me."

"Oh my gosh! That would be a major mistake, Alice," said Zen. "The school bus is the ideal place for you to meet people, and the teachers will probably line up at the entrance to greet us and point us in the right direction. If your mother drops you off, you'll have no idea what to do."

I had to admit those were all good points.

Then Zen asked me to stay one minute longer, that he had "a little something" for me.

As he disappeared inside his house, I suddenly grew

very excited. I could not wait until the following morning, my first day of sixth grade. I definitely felt ready for middle school, and it was all thanks to Zen. I pulled the dirty beach chair over and sat under the huge old tree. I thought about the first time the two of us had met here in his front yard and how I had misjudged him. Sure, Zen was odd, but he was also generous and talented and nice. After all, look how much everyone at church loved him. Not to mention Yaz.

The front screen door slammed shut. Zen hurried down the steps holding something in his hand. He rushed over, gave me a ball of gold tissue paper, then plopped down in his ratty lounge chair.

"I made it a while ago, but I waited until today to give it to you."

I tore off the tissue, revealing the yellow shell I had noticed from his collection the day before.

"Is a yellow shell a happy shell?" I asked.

"Wrong, but good guess. It's a friendship shell," said Zen. He leaned forward. "Read the message inside."

I turned the seashell over and read aloud the tiny

letters written along the rim:

"A best friend is like a cupcake for the soul."

"Do you like it? I wrote it myself." Zen grinned. "I want to have a whole line of these quotable seashells at my total body salon, but only perky messages, you know, little pick-me-ups, categorized by cheery colors like yellow and violet and magenta!"

As usual, it took me a couple of seconds to catch up to Zen's way of thinking. It was like he dreamed out loud when he was awake instead of silently when he slept.

"I guess it sounds like a good idea."

Actually, I had no idea what the message in the shell meant, but it made me hungry, which reminded me of Pop's pizza. I stood to fold my chair and leaned it against the tree.

"I gotta get going before lunch gets cold. Thanks for the shell."

"You better hang on to that one, Alice," said Zen. "It may be worth something someday!"

And he was right. I had no idea just how valuable it would become.

chapter eleven

"Breakfast, Alice Bunt!"

That was my father, calling me for breakfast on my first day of middle school.

"Breakfast, Sophie Bunt!"

Now he was calling my mother.

"Breakfast, Einstein and Yaz Bunt!"

Somehow those two knew it was the end of summer. Together they circled my feet as I tried to move down the hall without stepping on their paws.

In the kitchen Pop whistled over the waffle iron as a plate of hot rocket waffles steamed on the kitchen table. His cheerfulness and the delicious, toasty smell helped calm my jittery nerves.

"Looking snazzy again, Al!"

"Thanks Pop," I replied, "but I don't feel too snazzy. I feel more like a messy ball of knots."

Speaking of knots, I had forgotten to braid my hair the night before, so it took about fifteen minutes to comb out all the tangles that morning. Then I didn't have as much time for makeup, so I skipped the mascara altogether since I stunk at putting it on. After brushing my teeth, I noticed a little stain on my BTS shirt, so I had a big wet spot where I tried to clean it off. And by then I was so nervous, I didn't even try to walk to the music in my head.

I didn't feel *snazzy* one bit.

Mom floated into the room, kissed the tips of my ears, and sat down across from me. She was wearing a navy blue suit and smelled, as always, sweet and flowery.

"You look even lovelier than you did yesterday, dear," she said, and added, "I'm so glad you're wearing your hair down."

I reached over and pierced a rocket waffle with my fork. It was difficult to do since Yaz was curled up in my lap and Einstein was planted across my green sneakers.

"I only have time for one waffle, Pop," I said. "Zen is

expecting me by seven o'clock at the bus stop."

Both my parents stopped what they were doing.

"The bus?" repeated Pop. "But there are high-school students on the bus. I thought we agreed that your mother would bring you to school, Al."

"I drive right by, dear, on my way to the train station." Mom bit her lip. "It will give us some quality time together."

I didn't know what to say. They seemed so worried, like I was getting a ride from car-wreck Travis next door.

"But I've never been on a school bus. And it's a great way to meet people. And Zen said the teachers would greet us and tell us where to go. I wouldn't know what to do if you dropped me off."

Mom stared at Pop. Pop stared at Mom. Then Pop pointed his spatula at the ceiling.

"You've made some excellent points. Let's give it a shot!"

"I guess I have to agree," said Mom. She smiled. "You're certainly growing up." Then she leaned toward me and whispered, *"I notice you're wearing the new lip gloss. It looks divine."*

It didn't feel too divine. My lips were already dry.

Within a few minutes Mom, Pop, Einstein, and Yaz were standing at the front door, waving and whimpering as if I were leaving for good.

"Have a great first day, Al!"

"Remember every detail, dear!"

As I hurried around the cul-de-sac, I noticed the King quads outside, identically dressed in checked jumpers. Today was their first day of kindergarten, but they were ankle-deep in the dirt next to the garage where Mr. King had tried to grow grass. All of a sudden, Travis screeched out of the Lees' driveway and whipped around the circle. His parents had bought him a brand-new Jeep to drive to high school. (The bus was definitely safer.) And there were Mr. and Mrs. Reed in matching dark suits and black briefcases, walking all goo-goo-eyed out to their empty minivan, hand in hand. If I were them, I wouldn't be so excited about filling that minivan with kids after moving in next door to the Kings.

Zen appeared at his back door before I even knocked.

He was wearing a barbecue apron.

"Surprise!" he sang. "Breakfast is almost ready."

I couldn't believe what I saw. The kitchen table, cleared of all the books and half-dead plants, was neatly set for two. At the center of the table was a vase filled with wildflowers. Oddly, the room smelled like an Italian restaurant.

"Please, Alice, have a seat," said Zen as he scurried around the kitchen. He placed a glass of orange juice in front of me and said, "Freshly squeezed."

"But Zen," I stammered, "what about the bus? Doesn't it come at seven o'clock?"

He flicked his hand. "I wanted you here early for the surprise. We still have a good twenty minutes until the bus arrives."

Suddenly, Babs hollered from another room, "Put a lid on it!"

Zen frowned, then reached into the oven with an enormous potholder. He pulled out a casserole dish and placed it on the table.

"I hope you love lasagna," he whispered. "I have it

every morning, heated slightly for just a few minutes."

Lasagna for breakfast?

Next he poured two huge mugs of cocoa and pushed a bowl of tiny marshmallows in my direction. I was still standing.

"Alice, *sit*," he insisted. "I promise we have plenty of time."

I sat on the edge of the old wooden chair, my backpack close to my feet. Zen took a deep breath and sighed loudly, like a tired parent. He untied his apron, revealing the most bizarre clothes I had ever seen him wear.

His yellow T-shirt looked old and worn. It was decorated with gold musical notes printed above the words *Groovin' to the Music*. He also wore giant sweatpants the color of mint toothpaste. A bright blue vest hung loosely at his sides, and on his feet were black sneakers.

He plopped down across from me and scooted in too close to the table.

"So what do you think of my BTS outfit?" He grinned. "The formal periwinkle vest contrasts with the ebony sneakers, drawing your attention to the philosophical words on my T-shirt, which are further highlighted by the serene green athletic wear. Did you notice that?"

I had definitely noticed.

"I'm trying to develop my own cutting-edge look, like all the major designers," he continued as he dragged almost everything on the table toward his plate. "I think it's essential if my total body salon is going to be successful."

I was speechless. How was Zen able to choose my outfit so well when he had no idea what looked acceptable on his own body? Didn't he read magazine articles about what *boys* should wear on the first day of middle school?

"Aren't you hungry, Alice?"

Actually, I was starting to feel a little nauseous.

"I already had breakfast, thanks."

"But I squeezed the orange juice by hand," he said. "It took at least fifteen minutes."

I picked up the juice and managed a sip as Zen sliced a square of lasagna. He asked me to pass the bowl of marshmallows.

"Have you already had your cocoa too?"

I paused in astonishment. "I don't think I'm allowed to have cocoa this early in the morning."

"Gosh Alice," Zen giggled loudly. "There's a lot of stuff you're not allowed to do!"

"*I said put a lid on it!*" Babs hollered again.

Just then, the bus roared to a halt at the corner of the street. The driver beeped his horn.

"Oh no!" wailed Zen. "We must be one of the first stops!"

We scrambled to turn off the oven, grab our backpacks, and race out the front door just as the driver was pulling away. I waved my arms while Zen whistled shrilly through his teeth until the driver slammed on his brakes. The red lights started blinking and the doors rolled open. My stomach flipped upside down as we climbed the steps, completely out of breath.

I followed Zen to a seat in the third row. From one quick glance I could tell there were about eight kids on the bus. Most sat alone, slumped over in silence.

Zen leaned over and whispered in my ear, still panting from rushing down the street.

"The youngest, like us, sit at the front. The high-school seniors are in back."

I noticed the driver was staring at us through the reflection of his huge mirror.

"Hey you!" he yelled. "Shouldn't you be back a few rows?"

Zen peered around, then pointed at himself and asked, "Me?"

"Yeah, how old are you?"

"I'm twelve, but—"

"Back one more row, buddy!" yelled the driver. "Seventh grade starts in row four."

Obviously, Zen didn't want to argue with a loud, scary bus driver with arms like two baseball bats. He tossed his backpack into the seat behind me, then wedged his way in front of my legs into the aisle. A few older boys snickered, causing Zen to flush a bit.

At the next stop, a group of older, really tall kids got on with one younger girl about my age. She smiled and slipped in next to me. She wore glasses and looked very familiar. Before I knew it Zen was whispering in my ear again.

"Rebecca Aulowitz from the beginning of the yearbook," came his airy voice. "Remember, she's not for you, a 3 at best."

I was kind of annoyed, because she seemed like the perfect person to talk to. She had a nice smile and didn't look like a fussy, prissy girl. In fact, she was pretty much dressed the way I would have dressed on the first day of school if Zen hadn't picked out my clothes. She wore a light blue shirt and gym shoes with her dark hair pulled back in a braid. And her cheeks were definitely not covered in blush.

The bus ride was long and stuffy, with a dozen more stops until we arrived at school. I was shocked by some of the high-school kids who got on and shoved their way back to the older section. Compared to Rebecca Aulowitz and me, the girls looked twenty years old. And the boys were loud and messy, and a few even had real beards and voices lower than Pop's.

Every seat was packed, some holding three people, except Zen's. No one sat with him. It was odd—no one even seemed to know him. Zen, on the other hand, had something to say about every person who passed. Several times he leaned forward and whispered instructional comments in my ear, such as, *"She's a solid 12, Alice, but has an irritating voice and sneezes too loudly."*

When we arrived at Sachem Regional, everyone pushed and shoved to get down the bus stairs. The older kids were supposed to let the younger ones out first, but they didn't. Once outside, I looked around for the teachers Zen said would greet us, but not one adult was organizing the crowd. For a minute or two, I couldn't even find Zen. So like everybody else I pushed and shoved across the driveway and through the front doors with the mob of middle-school students. Thankfully, the high-schoolers turned right and ambled down the hill to the other building.

The entrance opened up into a wide lobby. Several glass cases full of trophies lined the walls, and in one corner, there was a water fountain. That's where I spotted Zen. He was picking up the contents of his backpack.

"What happened?" I asked.

His face was red and blotchy, but he replied calmly, "A little mishap." Then he swung his backpack over his shoulder and said brightly, "Let's find our homeroom!"

Joining the crowd, we pushed into the cafeteria to check the homeroom lists, which turned out to be alphabetical by last name. We weren't together. In fact, I was in Room 3C (Abbott—Czarch) while Zen was on a completely different floor in Room 28F (Lange—Overon).

"At least we'll have cafeteria and the bus ride together," he said.

I studied the map of the school as Zen commented on the girls in my homeroom.

"Oh no, not Rebecca Aulowitz *again*." He made a squishy face. "But look, Alice! You have Haley Benson in your class. Remember, she's part of your clique, definitely a 17 like you. Make sure you talk to her and her friend, Yvette Mimmick. They're super popular."

All of a sudden the bell rang. This was the last time I would see Zen until lunch period. It was finally time for me to try out everything I'd learned about being a real middle-schooler.

Chapter Twelve

Almost every desk was filled in Room 3C. Kids were chatting and shrieking, and someone was throwing wads of paper. The homeroom teacher, Mrs. Wong, sat at the front studying the announcements. She didn't seem to mind the commotion. Near the back of the room I noticed Rebecca Aulowitz. There was an empty desk behind her. I didn't care what Zen thought about my popularity index. I headed straight for the vacant seat. Rebecca smiled.

Just as I settled into my chair, a group of girls in the next row turned and stared. They were evaluating my outfit.

"Cute belt," said the tallest one. "Where did you get it?"

"The Clothes Bug," I replied, trying to sound extra friendly.

The four girls, plastered in makeup and jewelry, reminded me of the mannequins at the mall.

"Are you new?" asked the same girl.

"I moved here a few weeks ago from Boston."

All four smiled and shifted in their seats.

"I love Boston," said a girl with enormous hoop earrings. "Practically every store in the world is there."

"My cousin goes to college in Boston," said the girl in the middle. She had small, black eyes, ringed with pink eyeliner.

The fourth girl didn't say anything. She looked bored.

"What's your name?" asked the tall one. Her hair was that silky blonde hair you see in magazines.

"Alice Bunt."

"I'm Haley," she said, tossing her ribbon of hair. "Wanna eat lunch with us?"

I was amazed. I had already made friends with Haley Benson. Zen would be so proud of me.

After homeroom, I tagged along with Haley and the girls to each class. In most classrooms we were organized alphabetically. This meant I got to sit either behind or next to Haley, due to our last names. So it was as if we were destined to be friends, except for one problem. I didn't know *how* to be friends with Haley.

Every time I tried to say something, she interrupted me and turned toward someone else. And when we ran into somebody Haley or the other girls knew, no one ever introduced me. In fact, they would chat away as if I didn't exist. But the moment classes changed, Haley made sure I was the one following her, as if we were inseparable. Sometimes she was nice, the way she was in homeroom, but mostly I felt like one of her fashion accessories.

And another thing bothered me. Whenever we entered the hallway all four girls immediately began gossiping. You would think they had been assigned to a special committee to pick everyone apart! They usually started with the teacher—"Mr. B. is *sooo* old they're going to fire him at the end of this year"—and then moved on to the boys—"Matthew smells *sooo* bad that the principal called his mother"—and ended with the girls—"Tamara's haircut is *sooo* horrible; I heard her grandmother did it!"

I figured it might have something to do with the first day back from summer vacation. They were *sooo* excited to see one another they couldn't help babbling constantly about everyone else.

By math class I had a first-day headache, the kind when you want to go home and never get out of bed again. On the first day of school it's always impossible to believe that there will be a last day of school. It seems as if the teachers will never know your name. And the textbooks are so huge (especially the math book), you can't imagine ever finishing them.

I was relieved to make it to lunch period. I grabbed the homemade lunch Pop had made for me from my locker and caught up with Haley and the girls. My pop made the best sandwiches, and I was starving.

"You brought your lunch?" asked Haley. "Nobody brings their lunch."

By "nobody" I immediately understood she meant that *nobody popular* brought their lunch. It looked like I wouldn't be eating Pop's fantastic sandwiches from now on, except on weekends. As we passed a barrel, I reluctantly placed the paper sack in the trash and followed the four girls through the cafeteria line. Luckily I had a couple emergency dollars in my pocket.

We wandered across the lunchroom, balancing our trays as we surveyed the crowd. Haley seemed to be searching for the perfect spot, but I had no idea what that would be. Up ahead I saw Zen eating by himself at one of the only empty tables.

I pointed with my tray and said, "Let's sit over there."

Haley stopped in her tracks. The other three halted.

"Geez, you *have* to be from out of town," she said. "That's Zen Malinowski!"

The others burst into laughter.

My palms grew sweaty. "Why, what's wrong with him?"

Haley leaned in and said, "He's only the weirdest, most revolting person in the entire school district. Why do you think he's sitting all alone?"

I spent the afternoon in a fog. It didn't make sense. Why did everyone at the Seacoast Spiritual Center treat

Zen like a celebrity? And how could he know so much about the latest trends and the right cliques when he was the most unpopular kid in the school? According to Haley, Zen had to be the *lowest* person on the "loner or leader" scale.

I, on the other hand, never cared about any of that stuff before moving to Oakville. Now here I was worrying about clothes, avoiding a nice girl like Rebecca Aulowitz, and throwing my pop's homemade lunch in the trash just to fit in with a group of gossipy girls.

Still, these girls were the only people I knew other than Zen. Even talking to him would be the same as holding up a sign that read: *Alice Bunt has no friends!* Next to that, following Haley around and trying to act like her felt safe.

As it turned out, Haley was on the same bus as Zen and me, number 4. I followed her to the second row. She scooted in next to a girl who had sat at our lunch table but never said a word to me. She could have been Haley's twin sister, tall with the same straight, golden hair.

"Hey Yvette."

This must be the other popular girl Zen had mentioned. She and Haley left barely enough room on the edge of the seat for me to sit down. When the two of them suddenly paused to gaze at some high-school boy strolling by, I jumped into the conversation.

"Hi Yvette, I'm Alice!"

Both girls turned and stared as if waiting for me to say something else. Yvette pulled a comb from her purse.

I pressed on. "Are you Yvette Mimmick?"

She stopped combing her hair.

"How do you know who I am?"

Of course, I couldn't tell her that Zen Malinowski had instructed me to make friends with her because she would most likely be a 17 on his magazine quiz. So instead I replied, "I think I heard your name at lunch."

"Must have been me," chimed in Haley. "Yvette and I have been best friends since first grade. Even our mothers are best friends."

"Even our fathers and brothers," giggled Yvette.

They leaned into each other and made silly grins. It

made me want to find a best friend.

Just as the bus driver stretched to close the door shut, Zen practically fell up the steps. The driver scolded him, warning him not to be late next time. I turned away and faced the girls as Zen hurried back to find a seat. My heart raced. I was relieved he didn't see me.

"Geez, I can't believe *he's* on our route again," Haley winced.

"Why are you complaining?" whined Yvette. "*He's* in my homeroom!"

At the same time they scooped pockets of air with both hands and hurled it out the window.

"Zen cooties!" they shrieked and brushed their hands like they had been digging in dirt. Yvette thought this was so funny, she almost slid off the seat.

I turned around. A couple rows back I spied Zen sitting alone in the seventh-grade section, staring out the window. On a crowded bus he had found the only empty seat.

A few people remained as the driver pulled up to the corner of Hemlock Trail. Haley and Yvette's stop had been two minutes earlier at the corner of Bear Hollow and Pheasant Acres. (*Bears? Pheasant?*) I rushed off the bus, like I had a doctor's appointment or needed to go the bathroom.

"Wait, Alice!" cried Zen.

I couldn't talk to him. Not now.

"Got to run!" I called, trotting backwards as I talked. "Great first day! Got to go! See you later!" And I scurried up the street as quickly as I could, barreling right through our front door.

It felt as if I had been away for a month.

Pop had my fave snack ready: homemade chocolate chip cookies, a glass of whole milk, and half an apple smeared in crunchy peanut butter. Without thinking, I wound my hair into a ponytail and whipped off the tight belt. Both Yaz and Einstein curled into my lap as I ate at the kitchen table. My headache was almost gone. I took a deep breath and smiled. It was wonderful to be home and be myself again.

"So Al, how would you categorize your first day?" asked Pop. "Stupendous? Pleasant? Disagreeable?"

Even though I would have categorized my first day as hugely disappointing and utterly confusing, I knew Pop would have jumped out of his skin if I said so. So I told him what every parent wants to hear.

"Better than pleasant," I said, "but not quite stupendous."

Pop kept glancing in my direction, grinning as he chopped celery for that night's dinner. I could tell he wanted me to say more, but I didn't feel like talking. Not only was I exhausted inside and out, but I was completely bewildered over the whole Zen situation. And I didn't want those feelings to ruin everything about school. After all, some of the actual classes had been promising, especially earth science.

The phone rang just as I ate the last bite of peanut-butter apple. It was Haley.

"You've got to come over to my house!" she said. "Yvette bought pink press-on fingernails and there are enough for all three of us."

For some strange reason, I was flattered that Haley had called. But I had been looking forward to my own kind of afternoon. First I would walk Yaz and Einstein, then Pop and I had plans to work on the go-kart. Press-on fingernails hardly compared with that. In fact, that was about the last thing on earth I would choose to do.

I hesitated, searching for an excuse.

"I don't know if my father can drive me over."

But Haley continued on as if she didn't hear me, gossiping about the way the Spanish teacher, Ms. Carlos, had glared at Yvette during a locker break when she was "only talking to a really cute seventh-grader."

And then something funny happened. The telephone was in the front hall, and from where I was standing, I could see myself in the mirror next to the coat rack. With my hair pulled back in a messy ponytail and my makeup worn off, I looked like a little nobody kid again. I thought of all I had done to get ready for middle school and how I had already become part of the popular crowd. A lot of people already liked me.

Then I thought about Zen. He didn't belong anywhere. He was so different, people thought he was "revolting." Not one person had sat or even talked with him at lunch. That's what happens when you're totally unpopular.

I decided I'd better do everything I could to fit in at Sachem Regional, even if I didn't feel like it.

"So are you coming over or not?"

"Huh?"

"The press-on nails?" Haley sounded annoyed.

"Oh, yeah. I'll be over in ten minutes."

chapter thirteen

It turned out Haley and Yvette lived next door to one another, and their gigantic houses looked exactly the same, just like every other home in their subdivision. I wondered what Zen would say about that.

Everything was super fancy. They even had a huge chandelier in the front hall. The place reminded me of a hotel, like no one really lived there.

Mrs. Benson didn't say anything to me except to tell me that Haley's bedroom was at the top of the stairs, second one on the left. I felt a little nervous walking up there by myself, like I was trespassing.

The second room on the left had loud music pouring through the door, so I knocked as hard as I could.

"*Get outta here*, Cooper!"

I cracked the door open and said in my new perky

school voice, "It's me! Alice!"

Haley turned down the music. "Geez, it's you. I thought you were my dumb little brother."

Yvette giggled.

"What are you doing?" I asked.

"Our toenails," answered Haley. She shook a tiny red bottle as hard as she could.

"Press-on toenails?" I thought press-on fingernails sounded bad enough.

Yvette rolled across the bed laughing as if that was the funniest thing she'd ever heard.

"Gross, no," replied Haley. "We threw those fake fingernails out. They didn't work at all."

"They were *really* gross," repeated Yvette.

Immediately, Haley and Yvette continued chatting where they had left off. I sat down on the carpeted floor and glanced around the room, trying to keep myself occupied. It was the girliest girl's room I had ever seen. Everything, like the walls and the little sofa, was white. The queen-size bed even had a canopy and drapes. Zen would have loved the place.

"So aren't you gonna paint your toes?" asked Haley. She was staring straight at me as if I had done something wrong. "I have just about every color there is."

I had never in my whole life used nail polish and had no desire to learn now. I figured if I stalled long enough, they would move on to a different self-improvement project.

"Could I use your bathroom first?"

"End of the hall," she said, "before my stupid brother's room."

The bathroom was like the rest of the house, formal with swirly designs and pale colors. It looked like a pack of beauty pageant contestants had decorated the whole place. I remembered watching a beauty pageant once and worrying about how I was ever going to look that grown-up and curvy. Haley's house gave me that same nervous feeling.

Next to the toilet was a stack of magazines. Immediately I recognized one of Zen's faves, *La Mode*. In fact, it was the issue he had used to determine my skin tone. I wondered what Zen was doing at that moment. Listening to Motown records? Painting a shell? Crimping his hair? Sipping lemonade?

All of a sudden I heard a crash in the next room. I washed my hands quickly and crept around the corner. A boy about my height stood in front of a mess of tracks and clips. A large sheet of instructions was propped up against the wall.

"What's it supposed to be?" I asked.

"A roller coaster," he said. "But I need a ladder, 'cause I keep knocking it over. It's too high."

I examined the mess.

"You should assemble it on its side," I suggested, "then lift it up at the end."

I grabbed the instructions and sat on the floor. Before I knew it, I was busy building a Deluxe Time Warp Gyro Coaster with Haley's nine-year-old brother, Cooper. Pop had bought me one just like it the previous Christmas, so I basically knew what to do. Cooper didn't seem to know who I was or why I was at his house, but it didn't matter. We were having such a blast that I didn't even notice a half hour had flown by.

"*Alice!*"

Haley and Yvette were slumped against either side of the doorway, their arms crossed.

"*What* are you doing?" asked Haley.

"Yeah, *what*?" added Yvette.

I dropped a piece of extra long space-travel track and stood up quickly.

"I, uhh . . ."

I didn't know what to say, but before I could explain Haley ordered me downstairs.

"*Another Life* started three minutes ago!"

She was referring to everyone's fave television soap opera, which, at the time, I knew nothing about. In fact, back in the city I had never known anyone who actually watched soap operas, except our old landlady. But she had to stay in her apartment all day and guard the building.

Haley draped her long legs across the entire sofa. Yvette sprawled across the matching love seat. Once again, I sat on the floor.

The moment the television clicked on, Haley said,

"Wendi Lynn is going to elope with that sicko, Pierre Beaumont."

"Definitely," Yvette agreed, "and he is *sooo* disgusting."

I was amazed. The two of them gossiped about the television characters the same way they gossiped about people at school.

I tried to concentrate on the show, but sitting through *Another Life* was even more boring than standing in a super-long checkout line at the grocery store the day before Thanksgiving. I couldn't believe all the popular girls did this every day. In fact, I was practically asleep when I heard Zen's name mentioned during a commercial break.

"Did you see what he was wearing?" groaned Haley. "Like, *a vest thingy*!"

"And that crazy *Groovin' to the Music* T-shirt?"

"He's *sooo* weird!"

My head began pounding away again, pulsing with mixed emotions. Part of me felt ashamed that I even knew Zen, but a much larger part felt angry I was allowing people to be so mean to him.

I don't know what got into me, because (despite that magazine quiz) I definitely wasn't a leader. Other than my parents, no one really ever listened to what I had to say. Not even my own dog—I almost always gave in and let Einstein ride in the stroller. But it was the end of the day, and I was tired of listening to the two of them pick everyone apart.

"Actually," I began, controlling the jitter in my voice, "Zen knows a lot about clothes."

Haley was eating from a bag of corn chips, which she hadn't shared with anyone. She practically choked on a chip.

"Zen *who*?" she asked. "Because you couldn't possibly be talking about Zen Malinowski!"

"He lives at the end of my street," I confessed.

Yvette screamed so loudly that Mrs. Benson poked her head in for a second to see if we had spilled soda on the furniture.

"Alice! Don't tell me that you're friends with him or something," Haley said. "Because, in case you didn't notice, Zen Malinowski is a total *freak*."

I looked away.

"And if you hang around him," added Yvette, "everyone will think you're a *freak* too."

That was it. I needed to go.

"Is it five o'clock already?" I asked, glancing at my watch.

Haley didn't offer to ask her mother to drive me home, so I pulled out my cell phone and called Pop.

"Geez, I can't believe it!" Haley snapped. "Talking about that creepola Zen made us miss the end of *Another Life*!"

Chapter Fourteen

Mom drove me to school the next morning for two reasons. First, I didn't want to have to deal with Zen on the bus. And second, Haley informed me that *no one* rode the bus to school, only home from school, as if that made sense.

As my mother stopped to turn right at the end of Hemlock Trail, there was Zen standing to the left in front of his house. I stared down at my lap.

"Let's offer him a—"

"No!" I interrupted. "This is supposed to be our quality time. Remember?"

We chatted all the way to school about the weather, baseball, and my new friends. But my mind was still back at the stop sign. I wondered how Zen found the courage to even get on the bus. No wonder he had had school-itis.

How could everything have turned upside down in one day?

In homeroom, I headed to the back, where Haley and the girls were sitting. I peered at Rebecca Aulowitz and smiled as I moved past her. She returned the smile. Just as I decided I would try talking to her, Haley grabbed my arm.

"You won't believe what Stephanie Jenkins said to Mrs. Wong two seconds ago!"

"Who's Stephanie Jen—"

But before I could get out three words, Haley was telling the girls how someone named Stephanie told our homeroom teacher, Mrs. Wong, that she had to run back to her house, because she forget to wear deodorant. They all thought it was the most hysterical thing they had ever heard. I glanced over at Rebecca to see if she was laughing, but she was quietly reading a book.

School was pretty much the same as the day before, except it seemed to go a little faster. And I didn't have a headache, probably because I knew what to expect. I now knew to follow Haley around but not to say anything, just giggle when everyone else did. If I was going to survive middle school, it seemed the best strategy was to put all my energy into schoolwork and forget about making real friends.

My plan worked pretty smoothly until lunch period. By then my stomach was in knots again. Not only was the cafeteria food horrendous, but I squirmed with guilt as soon as I saw Zen.

He was eating alone, of course, and sipping soup from the top of a Thermos. As Haley and the rest of us passed him, my palms grew sweaty.

"*Hey dork*," said Haley, loud enough for Zen to hear.

I lowered my head and rushed directly to our table as the girls burst out laughing. And as I attempted to eat my Salisbury Steakinator Grinder and cole slaw, I didn't allow myself to glance once in his direction. It was as if I had no choice in my own actions anymore. I tried to figure out how this could have happened, if this was life in the suburbs. I forced myself to take a bite of the slimy slaw and wondered if Zen or Babs had made the soup in his Thermos. I guessed it was chicken noodle soup and that it tasted delicious just like Pop's.

At the end of the day, Haley rushed onto the bus as I obediently followed her. She sat down and plopped her backpack between us, leaving me enough room to totter on the edge. Of course, she was saving the better space for Yvette. Suddenly Zen walked up. I hadn't even noticed him falling up the bus stairs, so I was totally unprepared to avoid him. He stopped and smiled timidly at me, obviously hoping to sit with us. I panicked and turned away.

"Seat *saved,* Malinowski!" said Haley. As soon as Zen passed, she snarled, "Geez, I can't believe he would even think he could sit with *us*. Were you talking to him or something?"

I shrugged as though I had no idea why Zen would try to sit with us.

Yvette slid in so abruptly I was crushed between the two girls like cream cheese smashed between two halves of a bagel. As I listened to them dissect the events of the day over the top of my head, I stared blankly at the seat in front of us, just as I imagined Zen was doing a few rows back. Middle school was harder than anything I had ever imagined. And so far, the trouble had nothing to do with the work.

This life was going to be pretty crummy.

Zen didn't call over to me when we got off at our stop. In fact, other than the folding bus doors slamming together, everything was quiet. After a few yards, I peeked back and watched him walk to the front of his house, much slower than his usual pace. His head and shoulders were slumped.

I felt terrible. And so confused.

As I dragged my feet up Hemlock Trail, the gray sky started to drizzle. I didn't care. I took my time. The rain was comforting.

Just past the bend in the road I stopped and studied each house on our cul-de-sac. I thought about my quirky neighbors, and a new warm feeling rushed through me. At that moment I wanted to hug each and every one of them. The quadruplets were comical the way they chased each other around and around wherever they went. The Reeds were sweet the way they held hands all the time. And even the Lees were lovable in their rude, selfish way. They were all simple to understand. There was nothing complicated about who they were.

By the time I reached our driveway, I was dreaming of one of Pop's delicious snacks. As the aroma of fresh-baked coffee cake carried me through the front door, Yaz suddenly escaped between my legs and raced down the street. I couldn't believe I'd let him slip by again! And it was really starting to rain buckets. This time I knew I couldn't call Zen to ask for help, so I tore after Yaz as fast I could.

I rounded the corner by the stop sign, faster than C.Y. himself stealing a base. And then I spotted Yaz. His long dark tail waved back and forth like a piece of tall grass just above the broken concrete steps at the back of Zen's house. I bounded across the backyard, under the clothesline, and over the piles of broken clay pots. Deep within the hollow staircase Yaz was standing in a small wire cat crate filled with a dozen open cans, all reeking of fish. I stuck my hand in and pulled one out: *King Karl Norwegian Sardines Packed in Olive Oil.* Another can read: *L'il Lucy's Pure White Tuna.*

I couldn't believe it! Zen had been luring Yaz all along, then trapping him in a crate!

That must have been how Zen found Yaz so easily the very first time he ran away. And that's why Zen ended up sitting calmly in his yard holding Yaz each time he disappeared. No wonder the two of them seemed to have a special connection. Zen was supplying Yaz with an endless feast of treats!

But why would he try to steal my cat?

Out of the corner of my eye I noticed the kitchen curtain close. In a flash, I knew that Zen had been watching me. Fuming, I yanked Yaz out of the fishy metal crate under the broken steps and stormed back up Hemlock Trail.

Chapter Fifteen

The second Mom arrived home from work that evening I asked to go to the mall. She was delighted and took it to be an extension of our quality morning talk. I, on the other hand, was on a mission.

I needed clothes, shoes, jewelry, hair accessories, and most of all makeup. I was going to do everything possible to fit in with the popular crowd. Haley and Yvette were right. There was almost definitely something wrong with Zen. That's why nothing about him made any sense.

And to think, he had been luring and trapping Yaz all this time!

At first my mother enjoyed my preteen shopping binge. I was anxious to try on anything and buy everything. But when I asked for eyeliner, she said it was inappropriate for an eleven-year-old. When I told her I was ready to get my ears pierced, she said that *she* wasn't ready. And when I informed her that *everyone* at Sachem Regional highlighted their hair, she pulled me aside to a bench near the fountain.

"Why are we really at the mall, dear?" she inquired. "Is there something you'd like to tell me about your new friends?"

I shrugged my shoulders and settled for hot pretzels.

That night, as I lay in bed, I considered redecorating my room. I couldn't possibly have anyone over from school with a baseball-themed border and bunk beds. And it was almost definitely time for me to get rid of the old Erector Set in the basement. I should also think about packing away my number 8 baseball cap and autographed mitt to save for my own kid someday. Plus, Pop didn't really have time to work on a go-kart . . .

"I like your tank top," said Haley the next morning in homeroom. "New necklace?"

"My mom and I went to the mall last night."

Rebecca Aulowitz was sitting in front of me as usual,

but this time I didn't smile at her as I walked to my seat. She was probably nice, but I decided I should ignore her from now on, like everyone else did.

I suddenly found it easy to join in on the gossip between classes. And to my surprise, people listened! I informed the girls of Rachel Leroy's purple birthmark, which I had noticed in the gym locker room. And no one knew that Mrs. Epping, the earth science teacher, wore a wig. But I'd known since startling her in the supply closet two days earlier.

"What about that weirdo Zen?" asked Haley one day at the lunch table. "You must have lots of juicy stuff on him since he lives at the end of your street."

I peered over at Zen, who was sitting alone as usual, spreading jelly on a large muffin. Ever since I'd found Yaz under his steps, I had avoided even looking in his direction. But now I was startled by how tired he appeared. His movements were slow and he didn't bother to look up from his food.

Almost everything about Zen was worthy of gossip. A boy who based his opinions on magazine quizzes, who painted messages in seashells, who listened to old-fashioned music, who attended an "earth-based" church, who feasted on hot cocoa and lasagna for breakfast, and who lured and trapped unsuspecting house pets. I could have easily filled an entire binder listing peculiar facts about Zen.

"Nope, not really," I mumbled. "He's pretty dull." Then I took a bite of my Spicy Popcorn Pork, the cafeteria special.

For a couple of weeks, I had no problem fitting in with the popular girls. I knew how to dress, which kids to ignore, which color lip gloss to use, when to giggle, and how to walk like I was the most important person in the hallway. And for short periods, I was able to continue the act at home.

"I'll get my own snack, Pop."

"But I made butterscotch toppers. They're still hot!"

"Too fattening."

"How about yesterday's chocolate-covered pretzels?"

"And ruin my complexion?"

But as the days went on, I grew more bewildered.

Each morning before school I added a little more makeup and felt less like myself. I was firmly planted in the popular group, so why wasn't I happy? In fact, I felt lousy. I missed video games and my batting machine. Instead, I had to concentrate on clothing catalogs and catching up on *Another Life*.

One morning I woke up ecstatic with relief. It was Saturday! No makeup, no gossip, no lunch period, no bus, no Haley and Yvette, no school. I jumped out of bed and grabbed the first T-shirt and shorts I could find. Without brushing my hair I stuck it in a ponytail and grabbed my Number 8 Red Sox cap, autographed mitt, and baseball. (I was grateful I hadn't packed them away in the attic yet.) The sky was blue and the air was clear—a perfect day to play.

Downstairs in the kitchen, I fed my pets and gobbled down a bowl of cereal. I noticed Pop watching me.

"Any plans today, Al?"

"Not really," I blurted between bites of Crunchy Oat Squares.

"I see you have your mitt and ball," he said, emptying the dishwasher. "We could play catch later, if you feel like it?"

"Sounds good," I said. "After I walk Einstein and Yaz."

As I stepped outside, a leash in each hand, I swallowed the breeze and soaked in the sun. I decided I wouldn't let myself think about school all weekend. I would just enjoy being the old me. Einstein immediately began whimpering. He wanted the stroller. And why not? I hadn't been paying enough attention to either of my pets during these past weeks.

I placed him gently on the cushion. "Comfy, little puppy?"

Yaz tugged on his leash. I knew he was still dreaming about the cans hidden under Zen's back steps. He could probably smell the leftover fish wafting up Hemlock Trail. But I refused to think about Zen. I was not going to let him ruin this wonderful day.

All of a sudden, the King quads charged out of their garage like a wild herd of ponies.

"Alice is pushing the puppy stroller!" Jessi whinnied.

The four girls galloped in our direction. Yaz crawled behind my legs. Einstein huddled into a ball.

"WHOA!" I yelled as loudly as I could. They bumped into each other as they came to a halt.

"Since it's such a nice morning, I will let each of you push Einstein *once* around the circle."

"Can I put on his bonnet?" asked Jacki.

"Can I hold Yaz's leash?" asked Jenni.

"No," I said firmly (just as Zen would have done, except I wasn't thinking about him). "You can stand in a straight line and wait your turn."

To my surprise they did it. Kindergarten must have been paying off. Juli went first. I stood in the grassy center of the circle holding Yaz's leash. I felt like one of those doggy obedience school instructors.

"That's right, Juli," I called out. "Keep it smooth."

Jessi was the best, guiding the stroller as if pushing her very own baby. As I walked over to tell her what a great job she had done, I heard a strange gravelly noise, almost like a bicycle riding on dirt. Then I heard girls giggling in the distance. I turned around and there, coming around the bend in the road, were Haley and Yvette. On electric scooters.

I was shocked. They had never been over to my house. Suddenly I felt guilty, like I had been caught doing something illegal.

"Geez, Alice!" Haley said. "*What* are you doing and *what* are you wearing?"

I glanced down at my clothes as I jerked the elastic out of my tangled hair.

"Oh, this?" I attempted to explain. "My pop is doing the laundry. He does it every Saturday. So I had to wear this old T-shirt."

"Your *father* does the laundry?" asked Yvette.

I glanced behind me and saw that the quads were no longer standing in a line. In fact, Jenni and Jacki were fighting over the stroller as Jessi tied the bonnet backwards over Einstein's face.

Haley frowned. "Who are all those bratty little kids?"

"I'm babysitting," I fibbed. "They're my neighbors."

Now Juli and Jessi were in the stroller with Einstein, making it too heavy to push.

"I don't know," said Haley. "It looked like you were *playing* with them?"

"Your *father* does the laundry?" Yvette said again.

At that moment Einstein escaped from the stroller and raced around blindly with the bonnet tied over his face. All four quads took off squealing after him. I grabbed Yaz and joined in the chase. We ran in circles behind my house, through my backyard, under branches, and around bushes until Pop caught Einstein. He untied his bonnet. The quads continued running and squealing toward the Reeds' lawn, where pregnant Mrs. Reed was trimming the grass.

"Thanks, Pop," I said, totally out of breath.

I gathered up poor Einstein, who was shaking almost as much as Kissy-Missy.

My father lifted a sheet from a basket of wet clothes. He clipped it to the clothesline.

"Ready to play catch?" he asked.

I turned around and looked toward the cul-de-sac. In the distance I saw Haley and Yvette gliding away on their scooters. I watched as their heads disappeared around the bend in the road.

"Maybe later, Pop."

And I went back inside the house.

Chapter Sixteen

That Monday morning was one of the hardest mornings of my life. I didn't feel like getting dressed or choosing jewelry or putting on makeup, but I did anyway. More than any other day, I didn't feel one bit like me, Alice Bunt. But at the same time, I felt too embarrassed to be the real me, Alice Bunt. I was taking so long to get ready that Mom poked her head in my room to ask if I was sick. I thought about staying home, but decided I'd better save it for when I really needed a day off. It seemed like things were only going to get worse.

As usual, Zen was standing alone in front of his house waiting for the bus. This time I didn't feel angry or guilty as we drove by. I felt sad.

In homeroom I forced myself to peer at Rebecca Aulowitz, but by now she didn't even bother to look up as I passed by on the way to my desk. She knew I had been ignoring her. I sat down and stared ahead at Mrs. Wong, our homeroom teacher. Like always, she was reading papers and correcting tests.

"Are you in la-la land, *Alice*?" asked Haley, jabbing me with her pencil.

I startled a little, then mumbled, "I'm kind of tired, that's all."

"From *playing* all weekend with those little brats?" she teased.

I scanned the class quickly to see if anyone had heard her.

"I'm only joking," said Haley. "Geez, relax! Yvette and I knew you were babysitting. That's why we left."

But she was right the first time. I had been playing. And I liked to play.

After Mrs. Wong made the announcements she passed out a couple of memos, including one about U-12 Soccer tryouts. At last! I was worried I had missed it. The flyer said the season was starting late due to the construction of new athletic fields. We were to meet at the town park on Saturday morning.

"Soccer?" said Haley, like she had gagged on a spoonful of cough syrup. "Does anyone really play *soccer* anymore?"

Then she and her gang of three giggled, as if they were far superior to all girls who actually had interests other than celebrities and soap operas. I folded the memo into tiny squares and tucked it away.

"Oooh, look!" Haley shrieked. "The Musical Medley auditions are in one week!"

I glanced down at the other memo, something about a talent show.

"Oh my gosh, we have to do this," said Haley to the others, who squealed in agreement.

I read further: *The Musical Medley is open to all students with general musical talent. Auditions will be held next Monday directly after school in the auditorium. Fill out the attached form and return to your homeroom teacher before auditions. Please contact the gym teacher, Mr. Lewis, for further information.*

"Alice? Are you in?"

The other three girls turned toward me exactly at the same moment and stared.

"Um, I don't have a musical talent."

Haley shrugged her shoulders.

"Oh. Too bad," she said with a fake smile.

The girls mumbled in agreement, then obediently turned back and began planning their audition.

Later, as we stood in the cafeteria line, I longed for one of Pop's lunches more than anything. I practically felt homesick for honey-smoked turkey with pickles and tomatoes and lots of mayo on an onion bun with chips, carrot sticks, a yogurt, and a big chunk of fudge. I didn't know if I could force myself to eat a Shredded Beef Wrap with Cheese Sticks.

I couldn't bear to hear everyone make fun of Zen today. So I steered clear of him as I dragged over to our usual table. I thought I might even choke up with tears if I looked at him. It wasn't Zen I missed, not really. Especially since I was still furious with him for practically stealing Yaz. What I missed was my old self . . . the

Alice who cared about people. The nice Alice.

How did everything become such a mess?

"*Alice*, are you sick or something?" asked Haley. "Because if you are, don't breathe on me."

During the last class of the day, earth science, I day-dreamed about what I would do all afternoon. I was so anxious to go home, you would think I'd been away at camp. After Pop's snack I would, of course, walk Yaz and Einstein. Then I would play video games—

I came back to reality when Mrs. Epping began re-viewing the Seven Natural Wonders of the World. About six months earlier, Pop and I had found a great website about them. I always thought the most impres-sive was the Great Barrier Reef off the coast of Australia. But then again, the Grand Canyon was phe-nomenal.

Haley leaned over and whispered loudly in my ear, "I think Epping's hairpiece is on backwards."

Even though I had been the one to inform the girls, I no longer thought Mrs. Epping's wig was one bit inter-esting. In fact, I felt annoyed that Haley had made me miss what the teacher had said about the fourth Natural Wonder of the World, Mount Everest.

"So?" I mumbled.

"*What* did you say?" Haley blurted loud enough for everyone to hear, including Mrs. Epping.

"Is there a problem, ladies?" asked the teacher. The entire class spun around and stared in our direction.

"Not at all, ma'am." Haley grinned and tilted her head. "Alice just informed me that her mother wears a wig!"

Everyone began to laugh as poor Mrs. Epping patted at her own synthetic hairdo.

"Now that's your mother's private business, Alice, isn't it?"

Just as I sank down into my plastic seat, there was a knock on the door.

"Enter please!" called Mrs. Epping.

It was Zen.

I practically gasped. The moment he stepped through the door a snickering, giggling current, like an electrical shock, rippled through the room.

"What is it?" she asked Zen.

"Ms. Redpath would like to know—" he began.

Snickering, giggling—

"I can't hear you!" Mrs. Epping strained forward. "Don't be shy, come all the way in."

I wanted to disappear. But something inside me made me stare, the way you watch something you shouldn't. As usual, Zen was dressed in a strange concoction of clothes, his white-blond hair wildly crimped. His arms were folded tightly across his chest. Little beads of sweat bubbled across his forehead as his face turned crimson red.

"Ms. Redpath would like to know if you have the overhead projector."

The class burst into laughter. Mrs. Epping turned sharply.

"Why is that so funny?" she demanded.

Everyone instantly grew silent, except Haley, who snorted, which sent the class into uncontrollable chortles once again.

"*Who* was that?" asked Mrs. Epping.

She looked straight in my direction. I couldn't tell if

she was accusing me or asking me. I glanced at Haley, who glared back, eyebrows raised. I stared down at my lap.

"I don't know what's gotten into this class today," Mrs. Epping said, and then shifted back to Zen. "Young man, please tell Ms. Redpath that Mrs. Delaney has the overhead in her classroom."

The door closed. Zen was gone. People whispered and wiggled in their seats. Mrs. Epping sighed loudly, then finished up her talk on the Seven Natural Wonders of the World as I studied the minute hand on my watch ticking down the seconds toward the bell.

"You almost got me in trouble!" snapped Haley.

We were rushing toward the buses. There was no point arguing with her. She was always right.

"I mean, what teacher would send *him* to deliver a message anyway?"

As we approached the front lobby a crowd was gathering in front of the trophy cases. Kids were yelling. Our bossy gym teacher, Mr. Lewis, pushed through to the middle.

"Out of the way people!"

"Oooh," Haley squealed. "Looks like a fight!"

The idea of a fight sounded awful. Of course Haley stopped to gawk, but I continued toward the exit. With each step I took I fell deeper into thought. Something had to change. This clique business was ruining my life. As soon as I got home I would devise some kind of exit plan, no matter how painful or embarrassing or—

"It's just that creepola Zen," said Haley, who had caught up to me. "I've had enough of him for one day."

Instantly my heart began to pound. My teeth clenched. I turned around and charged back toward the lobby, but Haley grabbed my arm.

"*Alice*, what's wrong with you? We'll miss the bus!"

Before I could think, I yanked out of her grip and shoved my way through to the front of the mob. The gym teacher was holding another boy's wrist up in the air, as if he were a policeman about to read him his rights. Zen was on the floor leaning against the wall. His nose was bleeding.

"Zen!" He didn't hear me.

"Move it along, folks!" yelled Mr. Lewis. "This is none of your concern!"

I pulled a pack of tissues from my backpack and hurried around to the other side.

"Here," I said and handed him a wad.

He looked up and smiled.

"Thank you, Alice."

"Geez, are you crazy?" screeched Haley, who had followed me the entire way. "Let's get out of here—just leave him!"

"*Ladies and gentlemen*," barked the gym teacher. "You are to proceed directly to your buses!" Then he picked up his gym teacher's whistle, which hung around his neck, and blew it hard three times.

I stepped out from behind Haley's tall frame and said loudly, "Excuse me, Mr. Lewis?"

The gym teacher stared down at me as if he were nine feet tall. His shiny, bald head reminded me of the golden dome on the state capitol building.

"This better be important, Miss Bunt!"

"My father is picking us up," I lied. "Zen and I have

to go to the library to work on a project today."

"Well, I'm afraid Mr. Malinowski is going to be A BIT DELAYED this afternoon."

"*Alice!*" said Haley. "Have you totally lost it?"

"That's okay," I said to Mr. Lewis, ignoring Haley. "I'll wait for him outside."

"Hmph!" Haley grunted as she wheeled around and, to my uncontrollable delight, stomped off toward the buses. Alone.

Thirty minutes later, Pop pulled up to the curb of Sachem Regional just as Zen exited the principal's office. His nose had stopped bleeding, but the center of it was bluish-purple. The school nurse had given him a bag of ice to stop the swelling.

"Thanks so much for calling your father, Alice," said Zen. "That was a fantastic cover," he chuckled, "going to the library."

Zen continued chatting as if it were the last day of summer again. He didn't seem to remember that I had not spoken to him in a month. Or that he had recently been punched in the face.

"Everything okay, kids?" asked Pop, a bit alarmed by Zen's injury.

"Just a little mishap, Mr. Bunt."

As we slid across the back seat of the car, Zen immediately launched into his latest magazine quiz. I said nothing. Reality had sunk in while I was waiting for him. And total shock had quickly replaced uncontrollable delight. The truth was I had recklessly completed my exit plan before ever *planning* it.

"This test can tell you, Alice, if you should date an artist or a scientist or a chef or almost any vocation! It seems very accurate."

Would anyone at school ever speak to me again? Did Haley have that kind of power?

Zen asked, "Why don't you come over and take the quiz?"

I had no idea what he was talking about.

"Huh?"

"A matchmaking analysis? Don't you want to know what type of person you should date?"

It took me a few seconds to figure out how to answer that. I could see Pop grinning in the mirror, but I didn't think it was funny.

"I'm not exactly dating yet."

This didn't stop him.

"Then do you want to learn how to read palms? There was an issue of *Celebrity Tips Digest* that tells you precisely how to do it. And it's all true!"

I turned my head slowly and stared at Zen. The ice pack was starting to leak. Plump drops dripped into his lap.

"Maybe another time."

Don't get me wrong—a part of me was relieved that we were finally talking. It was like I could breathe normally again. But, in addition to the fact that I had just dove headfirst into the pool of unpopularity, I thought it was very strange how Zen was acting as if nothing was wrong. Didn't he need to explain everything that didn't make sense?

Why was he was so admired at church and completely loathed at school?

Why did he wear such ridiculous outfits when he dressed me like a model out of a preteen magazine?

Why did he insist I make friends with the two girls who were meaner to him than to anyone else?

And, most of all, why did he lure my cat to a trap under his house?

"You have to at least come over and try my new yoga ball," said Zen. "Truly, it's improved my posture."

He was grinning ear to ear. Maybe there was no way of ever figuring him out.

"Thanks anyway." I peered in the mirror at Pop. "But I think right now I have plans to work on a go-kart."

Chapter seventeen

Pop had already attached the axles to the chassis. I was surprised that the go-kart was more than halfway done. It was mounted on blocks in the back of the garage.

"I thought since you'd lost interest in it, Al, I'd finish it and give it to you for Christmas."

I didn't know what to say. How could I begin to explain where I had been the past four weeks?

I picked up a wrench and tightened one of the bolts on the right back wheel. It felt good to put effort into something that I knew would turn out well.

"Pop? Why can't everyone just accept everyone else?"

My father grinned as he slid the dipstick back in the oil.

"Sounds like a simple question," he said, "but there isn't a simple answer."

"Well, what's the main reason?"

He thought about it for a minute, then straightened up and rubbed his hands on his dirty jeans.

"The way I see it, most people feel the need to follow others and be part of the crowd, because it's a safe place. Then there are a few risk-takers who are brave enough to be different and think independently." Pop paused to wipe his forehead with an old towel. "But obviously, a crowd has a much louder voice than one individual."

"That doesn't seem fair," I said, moving over to the left wheel. "Doesn't the crowd ever listen to the individual?"

My dad pulled a lawn chair in front of the bumper. He balled up a cotton rag and polished the metal.

"All the time, if the individual can find a way to be heard. That's not always possible—plus, it takes a wagonload of courage." Pop paused to examine his reflection. "But as the individual gets older, he'll see it becomes easier and easier to be an independent thinker. To find his true voice. And express himself."

"Like a father who stays at home and does the laundry?"

He beamed. "Exactly!"

Just then, the phone rang inside. I opened the door to the kitchen and guess who escaped? In a flash, Yaz flew past us and down the road. I couldn't believe it—after a whole month he still remembered! I let the message machine answer the phone, then trudged down to Zen's house to retrieve my cat. I thought about telling Pop why Yaz persisted on taking off, but I decided it was only fair to first ask Zen. After all, that's probably the advice Pop would have given me.

When I pulled Yaz out from under the broken concrete steps, to my surprise, the fishy smell was gone. I leaned in and poked around with my hand but found nothing. No more crate. Yaz mewed as if someone had forgotten to feed him dinner.

Once again, the kitchen curtains closed quickly. But this time I jumped up the stairs and knocked hard on the back door. I had to bang three times before anyone opened it.

"We aren't buying!" yelled Babs.

"I'm not selling anything! May I speak with Zen, please?"

"He's not here!"

"But I just saw him—"

"I'm telling you, girlie, he left! I was watching my *Andy Griffith* program when that nutty-as-a-fruitcake boy tears past the television set and out the front door. Then you start banging back here making me miss even more of my show!"

She slammed the door shut, which made Yaz dig his claws into my arm. That was more than Babs had ever said to me in one breath, but by the time she had said it, Zen was long gone.

The next morning I asked Mom to stop at the corner and pick up Zen on the way to school. I was back to wearing my normal outfit again, a T-shirt and jeans, and my hair was in a ponytail.

"Thanks for the lift, Mrs. Bunt," Zen said. He was wearing a tropical print shirt over red shorts. "Lately, my feet have been killing me. I think I need to buy those arch supports they advertise in *Body by Design.*"

As usual, he babbled all the way to school about everything from antioxidant vitamins to homemade fertilizer for pumpkin plants. Not once did he mention our strange non-encounter with Yaz at the back of his house. To Zen everything was hunky-dory, as long as you didn't talk about it.

When we pulled up to the front entrance of Sachem Regional, my stomach twisted into knots as usual. But these were a different type of knots. These knots worried that everyone would gawk at us or that someone would try to knock me down the way they knocked down Zen. I was used to being with the popular group. I had no idea how it felt to be totally unpopular.

As we walked through the halls Zen continued his colorful chatter, which now included a recipe for room freshener. I, on the other hand, kept a lookout for bullies and tormentors and closed-minded followers. But to my relief nobody seemed to notice us.

"See you later, Alice!" chirped Zen. He bounced up

the stairs to his homeroom . . . as if we did this every day.

I forced myself to remain calm as I entered Room 3C. As usual, everyone was talking and some boys were throwing wads of paper. Mrs. Wong sat at her desk reading memos and correcting tests. Everything appeared normal as I slipped back to my usual seat. I glanced at Rebecca Aulowitz, but she didn't look up. She must have assumed I was still ignoring her. Or perhaps she was ignoring me. I wouldn't blame her.

Just as I slid into my chair, feeling convinced that everything would be fine after all, Haley whipped around.

"Seat *saved*!"

"But I always sit here."

"Not anymore," she snapped. "Didn't you get my message on your answering machine? I decided to rearrange the homeroom seats in this corner."

Obviously Haley wasn't in charge of the seating chart. In homeroom you were allowed to sit anywhere any day of the week. But Haley seemed to have more control over the class than Mrs. Wong did, so I realized it was probably wise for me to make a change. I searched the room and saw a few empty desks in the opposite corner. I picked up my books and moved away without glancing back. Some of the girls sneered.

"By the way, Alice—"

I turned back for a second.

"*Nice* outfit!"

It seemed like the entire class laughed hysterically.

So this was how it felt to be unpopular.

Of course, due to our alphabetical seating assignments I had to sit next to Haley in almost every class. Each time I slid into my chair she recoiled from me as if I were toxic, followed by a gaggle of giggles from the other girls. But I knew surviving class time wouldn't be the worst part. The biggest test would be the cafeteria.

I had asked Pop to make my lunch. Since I was no longer part of the popular clique, nobody would care if I carried a paper bag. But more importantly, I didn't have to buy that disgusting food anymore. No more microwaved Broccoli Puffs or fried Fish Fingers for me. At least I could look forward to a delicious sandwich.

On the other hand, I no longer had anywhere to sit. I lingered at my locker as long as I could. After the halls had completely cleared I peeked into the lunchroom. Right away I saw Haley and her gang crossing the cafeteria with their trays. As they passed Zen's empty table I could tell Haley said something horrible to him.

Just as I had felt the day before, a completely new strength stirred inside me. It was a feeling I had never experienced before living in Oakville. Once again, I boiled over with courage and marched directly over to Zen.

"May I sit here?" I asked too loudly.

He practically choked on his smoothie.

"Alice!" Zen coughed. "Please sit down. Would you like a deviled egg? They're good but I'm afraid I made them a bit too peppery."

He had a plastic container crammed with six egg halves, the creamy centers smeared all over the sides. He also had a bag of pistachio nuts and a huge cupcake.

"It looks tasty, but Pop packs a great lunch." I was still talking too loudly, and I noticed my hands were trembling.

At that moment another voice asked quietly, "Is anyone sitting next to you?"

I couldn't believe it. Rebecca Aulowitz!

"It's kind of noisy on that side of the lunchroom," she explained, pointing generally toward the windows.

I glanced immediately at Zen, worried he'd get some dumb idea from that "Loner or Leader" magazine quiz.

"Deviled egg?" he offered.

"No thanks," said Rebecca. "I brought some yogurt and a salad."

I was excited! Here I was, finally making my own choices, and it was working. A little rocky, but definitely promising. Perhaps this life would be okay after all.

"You're on our bus," I said awkwardly, just to start a conversation. But before she could respond, a Fish Finger sailed through the air and landed in Zen's container of eggs.

"Don't feed the animals!" someone yelled out. I

twisted around. Haley waved and made kissy noises. When I turned back, three more nuggets hit Zen's cupcake.

"Is there a *problem*, Mr. Malinowski?"

Out of nowhere that bald, bossy gym teacher, Mr. Lewis, appeared. His arms were crossed and he was glaring at Zen, like he had broken the law.

"This delicious delicacy slipped through my hands," Zen joked. His face was as red as his shorts.

I decided this was it. It was time our individual voices formed a group and spoke up against the crowd. Pop was right—it took a lot of guts—but it was now or never. I turned around and pointed at Haley's table.

"*They* threw it at us, Mr. Lewis," I reported. "Those girls over there threw four Fish Fingers."

But instead of righting the wrong, instead of marching over to Haley's table and reprimanding *them*, the gym teacher seemed perplexed. He raised his eyebrows and tilted his head. Then he smiled and pounded Zen's back, as if it were all a fun-loving prank.

"Let's make sure it doesn't happen again," said Mr.

Lewis. He winked at Rebecca and me. "Keep an eye on this guy, ladies!" Zen frowned and looked down at his lap.

I couldn't believe it. It was so unfair.

As Mr. Lewis strolled away, shaking his keys, Rebecca mumbled, "I hope his wife cooks fried Fish Fingers for dinner tonight—if he even has a wife."

Zen slapped his hand over his mouth and laughed.

Rebecca added, "Can you imagine what *his* kids are like?"

"I bet they all wear whistles and line up to go to the bathroom," said Zen.

Even though I was still steaming, I had to laugh too. It felt so good to laugh at something that was actually funny for once.

Chapter eighteen

Life hugely improved after lunch, because now I was friends with Rebecca. Luckily, her last name placed her just two assigned seats before mine. The only bad part was we were separated by Haley.

During our final period, earth science, Rebecca snuck a note to me. She was extra careful passing it behind Haley's back (and sour expression). The note read: *Want to sit with me on the bus today?*

It was one of the best notes I'd ever received in my entire life. I was so happy, I barely noticed Haley's nasty expression when the bell rang and I bumped into her chair.

Rebecca and I laughed and leaned into one another as we rushed to our lockers, then out to the bus line. At one point, Yvette tried to "accidentally" trip me with her backpack, but I jumped right over it as if it didn't exist. It was like I was getting the chance to start school all over again.

Just as we found an empty seat on the bus, Zen appeared.

"Is this spot saved, Alice?" he asked.

Rebecca and I scooted over. "Plenty of room!"

As it turned out, the bus was so noisy that we barely heard Haley and Yvette's mocking cracks. They were only a couple seats ahead of us, but they could have been sitting forty rows away. Like Zen and Rebecca, I learned to ignore *them*. I decided life at middle school was much easier for individuals if they stuck together.

Rebecca's stop was right before ours. As she jumped down the steps and waved "so long," I remembered that first bus ride when she sat with me. She seemed exactly like the kind of person I wanted to get to know in Oakville. And if it hadn't been for Zen and his magazine quiz, Rebecca and I could have been friends all this time. Suddenly, I felt confused again. There was so much Zen and I needed to talk about, but it seemed impossible to discuss anything with him deeper than facial pores.

"Oh Alice, I've been meaning to ask you!" said Zen, as the driver pulled up to Hemlock Trail. "Do you want to see my new hypnosis medallion? I can put you to sleep within sixty seconds and have you confess all your deepest secrets."

"Does it really work?"

"I tried it on Babs during a commercial break when she was watching *Andy Griffith*, and she confessed that she couldn't stand Aunt Bee and her homespun advice."

That's when I got a great idea.

"Sure, why not," I agreed. "But only if I can try it on you as well."

Zen's bedroom was a wreck. Worse than the first day I saw it. Once again his clothes flowed out of his closet and flooded the entire floor. His bedspread was in a ball tangled up with the pillows. Three of his Motown posters drooped over, barely taped to the wall. And cardboard boxes, filled with magazines and shells and assorted junk, took up the rest of the space.

"Snack's ready!" Zen sang. He entered the room carrying a tray. He offered more of the same cupcakes he had at lunch, as well as two glasses of lemonade with ice.

"What do you think of my new shutters, Alice?"

I hadn't noticed anything new in all the mess, but there they were. Two mismatched shutters framing either side of the window.

"Are you still redecorating?" I asked politely.

"It's an endless job," he replied as he stirred his lemonade with a straw.

I peered up at the glass shelf above his bed. There had to have been ten more shells added to his collection. They were all painted either blue or green. No more yellows.

Upon finishing his cupcake, Zen brushed his hands loudly.

"Okay," he said, his mouth still half full. "I'll hypnotize you first, so you can see how it's done. Then you can do me."

He pulled a shiny gold chain with long links from a white silk pouch. At the end of the chain was a royal-blue plastic pendant, as big as a silver dollar and cut like a diamond. Also inside the pouch was a tiny booklet with instructions. Zen quickly skimmed the first few pages.

"We need to sit across from one another," he began, "so you sit on the bed. I'll get a chair from the kitchen."

A minute later we were settled and ready to begin. Zen swung the chain back and forth. He held it high so I was staring right at the medallion.

"Don't move your head, Alice. Follow the *power of blue* with your eyes alone, back and forth, back and forth."

After about twenty back-and-forths my eyes were starting to ache.

"The *power of blue* is making you sleeeepy, very sleeeeepy," he said softly as the swinging slowed down. "By the time I count backwards from ten your eyes will be closed."

I couldn't wait to close my eyes. They were stinging so much.

"One!" he finally said, and I shut my eyes tight.

Zen chirped with delight. I think he was surprised that it seemed to be working.

"Can you hear me, Alice?" he asked in a ghostly voice.

"Yes," I replied in my own ghostly voice.

"What is your naaaaame?"

I fought to keep myself from smiling and answered, "Aaaalice."

"Where do you liiiiiive?"

"Hemlock Traaaaaail."

I thought he was supposed to be asking me my deepest, darkest secrets.

"What is your laaaaaast name?"

This was getting boring.

"Buuuuunt."

If he didn't ask a good question soon I was going to have to scratch my nose, which was super itchy.

"Who's your best frieeeeeend?"

Oh boy—I wasn't ready for that one.

"I'm not sure yeeeeeeet."

Zen didn't say anything so I cracked open one eye. He was pressing his forehead like he was trying to think up another good question.

"What's your favorite coooolor?"

This was getting ridiculous. I scratched my nose and pretended to snap out of it on my own.

"Oh, that was so strange," I said, rubbing my eyes. "I could hear you asking the questions, but it was like I had no control over what I was going to say!"

"Really?" Zen asked. "Try it on me."

So we switched places. I swung the chain and chanted the instructions until it appeared that he was truly asleep. Either Zen was very open to hypnosis, or he was a much better actor than I was.

"What is your full naaaaame?" I asked.

"Zenithal Stevie Wonder Malinooooowski."

Zen swayed a little when he answered. I was worried he might tip over.

"What's your fave maaaaaagazine?"

"Definitely *Body by Desiiiiign*."

Okay, enough fooling around. I was really hoping he

would confess the truth whether or not he was actually hypnotized.

"Why did that boy at school give you a bloody noooose?"

Zen squeezed his eyes tight. He answered quietly, but not in a ghostly way, "Because I told Ms. Redpath that he cheated off my test."

I pressed on.

"Well, why do you dress so," I paused, "*differently* from everyone eeeeelse?"

He answered just like the last time. "I told you before, I'm developing my own unique style, like all the big-name designers in the magazines."

His style was unique all right.

Suddenly, Zen's bottom lip started to quiver, and he seemed to be having a hard time keeping his eyes closed. I was getting worried. I didn't want him to break down and cry, so I spoke more quickly.

"Why did you tell Alice to be friends with such mean giiiiirls?"

He frowned, then bit his lip hard. "They're popular. I

thought you could be popular too."

Why did he think I cared so much about being *popular*? I just wanted to fit in at Sachem Regional, not rule it.

Now for the really big question. I hoped he could hold it together to answer.

"Why did you lure Yaz to a crate under your staaaairs?"

At that moment, Zen scratched his nose and rubbed his eyes.

"Oh my gosh," he sighed as he forced himself to yawn, "that *was* strange. I know you asked me all this stuff, but I can't remember what it was."

He quickly shoved the medallion back in the white pouch and changed the subject.

"Hey, do you want to exfoliate your elbows? I read if you grind up oatmeal, honey, cider, and almonds it makes the best callous scrub."

"No thanks," I said. "I promised Pop I'd be home by four so we can work on the go-kart."

It was true. I did tell Pop I wanted to install the ignition today. But there was something else. I felt uncomfortable around Zen. It wasn't that he had changed in any way from the person he was before, but *I* had changed. I needed good, honest friends I could trust. Not fake, gossipy friends like Haley and Yvette—and not friends who steered clear of the facts whenever they felt uncomfortable. I was glad Zen had finally told the truth about some things, and I was impressed he had stood up for himself when that kid cheated off his test. But until he explained why he tried to trap Yaz, I couldn't completely trust Zen.

Chapter nineteen

The next morning Rebecca joined me on the other side of homeroom, far from Haley and her crowd. As soon as she sat down, she pulled out the memo about soccer.

"Are you going to try out?" she asked.

I couldn't believe it. I had forgotten all about soccer since Haley had ruined it for me with her snobby remark.

"I'd like to, but I lost the form." I didn't want to admit that I had really folded it up into tiny squares and thrown it away.

"Well I am," she said cheerfully. "I've played soccer since kindergarten."

"Me too!" I told her. "Have you seen any professional games?"

"Only on TV. But my Mom and I see the Red Sox play

baseball in Boston whenever we can. Sometimes she gets tickets at work."

"Are you kidding?" I squealed. "Baseball is my absolute fave sport in the world."

I could have jumped up and hugged her, but at that moment a wad of paper bounced off the back of my head.

"Haley," Rebecca informed me.

I turned to see the four girls in a huddle. Haley peered over her shoulder and glared in my direction.

I picked up the ball of paper.

"Don't bother reading it," said Rebecca. "You should throw it away."

Rebecca was right. Nothing good would come from reading it. Haley just wanted to make me feel bad about myself. So I tossed it perfectly into the trashcan on the other side of the room by the door.

A couple of boys near us applauded and called out, "Three points!"

Then I asked Mrs. Wong for a new soccer form.

At lunchtime, Rebecca and I plopped down across

from Zen at our table. He was eating bologna and tartar sauce on a huge, bulky roll. Rebecca and I continued our chat about baseball (the best batting average), then moved on to dogs (the best breed), and finally, video games (the best system).

Zen said nothing until he finished his entire lunch. He wiped his face carefully, then commented, "I don't know why it is you never see professional sports teams wearing pink. It's actually a very motivating color."

I glanced nervously at Rebecca to see her reaction. What if she thought Zen was nuts like everyone else did?

"Some teams wear a pinkish-red color," she replied, "like maroon."

"Not maroon, I'm talking about bubble-gum pink," said Zen. "It's bright, it's cheerful, it's eye-catching. *Body by Design* lists true pink as one of the five healthiest colors."

I couldn't believe we were having this conversation. I changed the subject.

"Did you know that Rebecca and I are trying out for

the soccer team?"

"*Why?*" asked Zen. He made his squishy face.

"Because it's so much fun!" said Rebecca.

"And great exercise," I added.

"And so much fun!"

"And competitive—"

"Okay, okay!" Zen cut us off. "Whatever you say. First go-karts, now organized sports. I just can't imagine getting all dirty and sweaty on purpose."

Rebecca and I swapped desserts and planned our entire Saturday around the soccer tryouts. We discussed what to bring and where to meet. Then we debated over our fave international soccer players. By the end of lunch, we had assembled the world's best soccer team . . . and Zen had folded a paper napkin into an origami sailboat.

Before last period, Rebecca asked me over to her house to practice shooting goals. I thought it was a great idea.

On the way to the bus line, Zen caught up to us, which was unusual. He was always one of the last people to get on the bus.

Out of breath he asked, "Do you two want to come over and decoupage milk bottles? I learned how to do it in *Custom Crafts Magazine*."

"Day-koo-what?" I asked as we climbed up the steps.

"Don't tell me you've never heard of decoupage, Alice? It's amazing. When you're done, it looks exactly like stained glass."

The three of us slipped into a seat.

"My aunt decoupages everything," said Rebecca. "Lamps, tables, photo albums."

"Your aunt's right," said Zen. "The article said you can decoupage almost anything!"

Just then, Haley called out, "Why don't you *decoupage* your mouth!"

A bunch of people laughed, which made the insult harder to ignore. It also made it more difficult to tell Zen, who was as red as my backpack, that we already had plans.

"We kind of agreed to practice soccer today."

"You could play goalie?" Rebecca suggested.

"No thank you," replied Zen, his enthusiasm shattered. "I need to start on my milk bottle."

Rebecca's house was almost as small as Zen's, but very cozy. Everything was wood, so it reminded me of a cabin in the forest. Her mother had hung dried flowers and herbs from the ceiling and the kitchen smelled like homemade bread.

In a glass room in the back of the house, Rebecca had two big colorful parrots named Peek and Boo.

"They can live as long as eighty years," said Rebecca. "And Peek can say more than fifty words."

"What if they live longer than you?" I asked.

"I hadn't thought about it," she said. "Do you want to be their legal guardian?"

"If they don't mind cats and dogs."

Beyond a small lawn, her backyard was woodsy with rusty pine needles covering the ground. Even though it was warm outside, the smell of pine reminded me of Christmas. The only open area to play was directly behind the house, so Rebecca had drawn a goal with a piece of chalk across the cement foundation.

"Your mom doesn't mind you kicking the ball against the back of the house?"

"She used to mind when her lily plants were there, but she transplanted them so I could practice."

We kicked the ball around, passing back and forth to warm up.

"What about your father? Does he mind?"

So far Rebecca hadn't mentioned her pop, and I'd seen no sign of a third person around the house.

"My parents divorced when I was a baby. My father remarried and moved to Idaho. He has three other kids now."

She said everything calmly, as if she were talking about someone else. But I knew it had to be hard not to have your father around. And for him to have a whole other family.

"Idaho? That's so far away. Do you ever visit him?"

I passed the ball to Rebecca and she slammed it into the chalk goal.

"Once a year, in the summer, I go out there for two weeks."

I couldn't tell if she wanted to keep talking about her father, so I changed the subject.

"Do you have any other pets?" I asked.

Rebecca smiled mischievously. "I have a rat in my bedroom."

I stopped in my tracks. "Can I see him?"

Her bedroom was at the end of a short hall, right next to her mother's. It reminded me of my old bedroom in the city. The wallpaper was old-fashioned with faded roses, but it didn't matter. Rebecca had covered it with fantastic posters of sports teams and wild animals.

One side of her room had a wide picture window with a deep windowsill. That's where Mr. Lincoln, the rat, lived in his cage.

"He's so big," I said, not sure if I liked him or not.

His tail was long and pink like a worm. He stood on his back legs and looked directly at us.

"I adopted him from my second-grade class at the end of the year," explained Rebecca. "We had two rats, Abraham and Mary Lincoln. Another kid took Mrs. Lincoln."

It turns out rats are very smart, much brighter than other rodents. When Rebecca rang a bell on the outside of his cage, Mr. Lincoln waddled over for his dinner, his whiskers twitching. He could also hop on his hind legs, and she was in the process of training him to walk a tightrope.

When Pop picked me up I couldn't believe it was already time to go.

"I haven't seen you this happy, Al, since the day we moved to Oakville," said Pop.

I smiled ear to ear and replied, "That's because I think I finally met my best friend."

But as soon as I said that, I thought of Zen's yellow shell sitting on my desk at home and felt guilty. It didn't make sense. Zen and I had absolutely nothing in common, and most of all, I didn't really trust him. How could we ever possibly be *best* friends?

Chapter twenty

On Saturday morning, I awoke to the smell of rocket waffles. I wondered what the special occasion was and then remembered—soccer tryouts! As Yaz, Einstein, and I searched through my closet for shin pads and cleats, I thought about Rebecca. Why hadn't I asked her to spend the night? We could have had rocket waffles together before soccer.

The King quads were up already and playing in the cul-de-sac. I could hear them squealing through my open window. As I sat down on the edge of my bed to tie my cleats I peered out to see what they were doing. These days they were obsessed with playing scarecrow tag. But at the moment they weren't playing any games at all. They were running in circles around Zen, who was hurrying toward my house. He carried his umbrella in one hand, an envelope in the other.

He stopped in front of our driveway and said something firmly to the quads. The four of them instantly ran squealing back to their yard. He may have problems at middle school, I thought to myself, but Zen certainly knows how to handle that group of girls.

I waited by the window for him to ring the doorbell, but he didn't. The next thing I knew Zen was practically running back down Hemlock Trail, the envelope no longer in his hand. I raced down the stairs, along with Einstein and Yaz, and found the letter on the front carpet under the mail slot. The envelope was pale yellow and smelled lemony.

"Man your stations," Pop called from the kitchen. "The rocket waffles have landed!"

"Be right there!" I called back.

Mom descended the stairs wearing a cotton bathrobe and matching slippers.

"Who's that from, dear?" she asked as she kissed the tips of my ears. She smelled as soft as her bathrobe felt.

"Zen," I replied.

The front of the envelope was addressed to "A. Bunt"

in neat handwriting.

"Looks like an invitation," said Mom.

"May Day!" Pop called louder. "The engines are cooling down too quickly!"

"We better eat," said Mom.

I put the envelope on the hall table and hurried off to the kitchen. I figured I'd read Zen's invitation after the rocket waffles, but by then, we had to rush off to soccer.

Tryouts were great for two reasons. First of all, everyone made the team. They had sixteen spots and only sixteen girls tried out. And second of all, just a couple of other girls were better than Rebecca and I, and not by much. In fact, we would probably score a 17 on a scale of 1 to 20 in one of Zen's magazine quizzes.

Rebecca's mother, Mrs. Aulowitz, gave me a ride home after practice. I invited them inside.

"Won't you stay for lunch?" asked my mother. "Jim is grilling hot dogs."

Mrs. Aulowitz hesitated. Like Rebecca, her mom was also a bit shy.

"Please, Mom?" Rebecca pleaded.

Her mother smiled. "That does sound good, thank you."

I am not exaggerating when I say that I had one of the best Saturdays of my life. After I pried Rebecca away from Yaz and Einstein, I showed her my baseball mitt autographed by #8 himself, as well as my Yokemat Cards, my Biker Buddy, and my electric drumsticks. Rebecca loved my navy-blue baseball-themed bedroom and said she wouldn't change a thing. We charged down to the basement, fooled around with the Erector Set, and played a video game. Rebecca couldn't believe how long our rec room was. She did fourteen cart-wheels from one end to the other.

Before we knew it Pop hollered down the stairs, "Lunch, girls!"

The five of us ate on the patio. I was glad Mrs. Aulowitz seemed to be more relaxed. And Yaz and Einstein were practically glued to Rebecca. I was smiling so hard inside I felt I might burst. Imagine, just a week ago I was suffering under Haley's rule in her kingdom of gossip and makeup. Somehow, I had found the courage to be myself.

This life was going to be pretty great after all.

"What's that?" Rebecca pointed toward the back of the garage.

My father had moved the freshly painted go-kart out into the sun to dry. It was tilted up on two wooden blocks.

"Pop and I are building that," I said proudly. "It's a go-kart."

"A real one?" she asked.

"Engine and all," said Pop.

"Where will you drive it, Alice?" asked Mrs. Aulowitz.

I hadn't really thought about it. "I suppose around the circle in front of my house."

"And Jim thinks they can make a trail in the woods," added Mom.

"Are you done building it?" asked Rebecca.

Pop and I laughed. We felt like we would never get the go-kart exactly the way we wanted.

"You're welcome to help us out," said Pop.

"Really?" Rebecca replied, practically jumping out of her skin. "How about now?"

"Can we, Pop?"

I was more than happy to share my dad with Rebecca. After all, he was about the best pop there ever was.

"I have a wonderful idea," said Mom to Mrs. Aulowitz. "Why doesn't Rebecca spend the night?"

Mrs. Aulowitz furled her eyebrows a bit. "I don't know. She rarely stays away from home—"

Then she stopped to watch Rebecca, who was holding Yaz and Einstein in her lap. Rebecca lifted their tiny paws and pouted, so that it looked like all three of them were begging at the same time. It was so funny I almost fell off my chair.

Mrs. Aulowitz grinned. "—but I think it's a terrific idea!"

The next morning, I awoke before everyone else. I dropped over the side of my bunk bed and saw that

Rebecca was still sound asleep. I wasn't surprised since we had stayed up until midnight watching a Godzilla movie marathon on channel 36.

As soon as Einstein and Yaz saw that I was awake, they raced around the room. I hurried them downstairs for breakfast. Pop and Mom always slept in on Sundays, so I crept as quietly as I could.

At the bottom of the stairs, I spotted Zen's letter on the hall table. I couldn't believe I had forgotten all about it. I quickly scooped out a cup of Doggy Munchettes for Einstein and a half-cup of Gourmet Cat Chow for Yaz. Then I opened the letter. The lemony stationery matched the envelope, but it wasn't an invitation . . .

Dear Alice,

i watched you and your family the day you moved in. i hid behind the juniper bush where the road curves. The three of you fit together so precisely, like three pieces of a puzzle. Even your pets looked happy. So i just had to figure out a way to get to know you. Believe it or not, i recently had a cat of my own. Are you surprised? i called him Marvin, after the gifted yet tragic Motown star, Marvin Gaye. Anyway, Marvin was a stray who wandered into my yard when they were bulldozing your street. He was terribly skinny and cried for hours. As you can well imagine, Babs refused to let him in the house. So i set up a kitty fort for Marvin under the back steps. He slept there every night until four months, one week, and six days ago. For some reason, he never came back. i couldn't bring myself to remove the crate or leftover cans of fish, just in case Marvin needed a place to stay sometime in the future. Then i met you that Saturday when it was really hot and Yaz disappeared. As soon as you ran off in search of him, i had a hunch he'd headed straight for my kitty fort. You were so happy when i found him, i decided Yaz was the best way to get to know you. So i kept the kitty fort stocked, thinking if your kitty liked me then you would like me. And it worked! Then i realized that if the popular kids at school liked you, they would like me, because you liked me, because kitty liked me. But that part didn't work. Not at all. And now i only care if you (and Yaz and even Einstein) like me. Sorry.

Hopefully still your friend,

Zenithal Stevie Wonder Malinowski (Zen)

I checked the clock on the wall. Eight-thirty. I raced upstairs and woke Rebecca. It took her a second to remember where she was, but then she shoved her hair out of her face so she could see my bedroom.

"Do you and your mother go to church?" I asked.

Still groggy, Rebecca replied, "We go to temple, sometimes."

"What kind of temple?" I inquired, as if I were now an authority on religion.

"The usual kind," she said, "with everyone sitting in rows and praying and the rabbi rambling on. It's pretty boring."

"Well, I *promise*, you've never been to a church or temple like the one we're going to this morning."

We washed and dressed, then served ourselves two

bowls of Crunchy Oat Squares. After slipping on our sweatshirts we climbed back up the stairs and tapped on my parents' bedroom door.

"C'mon in," Pop called quietly.

Mom was still asleep, but Pop was sitting up in bed reading the newspaper.

I whispered, "We're going to church with Zen."

"Again?" he murmured, sounding a little surprised. "Come home right after the service. I'm making pizza. Invite Zen, of course."

We raced out of the house and down Hemlock Trail. The quads chased us for a few yards but gave up as soon as we disappeared around the corner. We arrived just as Zen was closing Babs's car door.

"Any room for us?" I asked, panting and sweating a little from the sprint.

Zen was wearing his church clothes, a nice blue shirt and dark pants. He stared at Rebecca and me as if we were aliens who had landed in his front yard.

"Don't you have soccer tryouts or something?" he asked.

"That was yesterday," said Rebecca. "We want to go to your church!"

Zen broke out into one of his ear-to-ear grins.

"There's always room for more at the Seacoast Spiritual Center!" he exclaimed, practically glowing.

"Well, *get a move on it*!" yelled Babs. "If they're out of those vanilla crème-filled donuts, I swear, we're turning 'round and coming home!"

chapter Twenty-one

Rebecca insisted on sitting up front with Zen's grandmother. She had never been inside an old Volkswagen Bug. And to my amazement, she was able to carry on a conversation with Babs. It turned out they both liked to watch the old black-and-white TV reruns. I, on the other hand, hung onto the window crank to keep from getting carsick. And Zen, as usual, sang scales to warm up his vocal chords.

This time when we entered the SSC I really tried to figure out what was going on. Like before, everyone touched Zen, shook his hand, and hugged him as if he were something extra special. It was exactly opposite of the way he was treated at Sachem Regional. At school Zen was a loner. At church he was a leader.

"See how they love him here?" I whispered to Rebecca.

When the harpist began to play, everyone rushed to find seats in the Sacred Circle, except Babs. She dragged a folding chair over to the cocoa-hour table and planted herself in front of the pastries.

"Hear the voice that sings in you, it creates the world anew," sang Elder Brightstar as he entered from a side door wearing his light blue gown and plastic ivy. I got a little excited, like I was watching a familiar play.

Rebecca wasn't one bit shy the way she was at school. She enjoyed the clapping and chanting and twirling and chanting and stomping and chanting. At one point she even threw her flower in the Sacred Space and shouted, "Rejoice!"

I wondered what it was about this bizarre church that made everyone feel so normal.

Again, near the end of the service, Zen and the other Sacred Songsters, young and old, formed a stretched-out ring outside our circle. (It still reminded me of duck-duck-goose). As they pulled on their tie-dyed robes ,they swayed to the rhythm set by the harp. Then we swayed. Elder Brightstar swayed. The whole building seemed to sway.

Suddenly, Zen looked up at the ceiling and sang out loudly and dramatically, like he was performing on stage. A man, shorter and heavier than Zen, sang along with him. His voice was strong and smooth, reminding me of sweet, creamy chocolate. His bristly hair was as white as sugar. Then the rest of the Sacred Songsters chimed in. I didn't really understand the meaning of the lyrics (something about "the ocean in motion"), but the melody was magical and dreamy—as if whales could fly and doves could swim.

"That was Wintermoon!" said Zen, breathing hard at the end of the service. "Doesn't he have the purest voice you've ever heard?"

"I like your voice just as much," I replied and meant it.

"Really?!"

Rebecca agreed. "It's different from his, but just as good."

We poured ourselves hot cups of cocoa and followed Zen around the room. He introduced us to the rainbow of people milling about. One woman wore a black turban, another had pierced eyebrows. There was a boy in leg braces with his grandfather, who had a long, silver ponytail adorned with feathers. Like Zen, everyone was friendly and polite. Some of them even remembered me from before.

Then all at once, it became clear to me. Every one of these church members had something in common. They were individuals who heard and accepted one another. A crowd of individuals, not an individual crowd. I didn't know what it was they believed in at the Seacoast Spiritual Center, but I could see they believed in each other. Like the quote out front on the big round sign: *I have the right to respect what I am.* No wonder Zen loved this church so much.

In the distance I heard a faint honking. It grew louder and louder. It had to be Babs waiting in the Volkswagen Bug.

"Get a move on it!" she yelled as soon as the three of us exited the big red barn door. "*Andy Griffith* starts in ten minutes!"

"I'm sure you've already seen it twenty-nine times!"

Zen hollered back.

Babs honked again.

As we piled into the car, I suddenly had an idea. It was about that memo that was passed out at school. Not the soccer memo. The other one . . .

"You know, you should sing in the Musical Medley, Zen."

He frowned. "No thank you."

I clutched the window crank and stared straight ahead as we tore out of the parking lot.

From the front seat Rebecca asked, "What's that?"

"A popularity contest," remarked Zen.

"No it's not, it's some kind of a talent show," I told Rebecca, "but only musical talent. You can play an instrument or be in a band *or sing*."

Rebecca whipped around in her seat. "Zen, you should sing!"

The more I thought about it, the more excited I got.

"No offense, Alice, but it's a horrible idea," declared Zen.

"Are you kidding?" I grabbed the door handle as Babs

veered left through a yellow light. "It's the best idea I've ever had!"

After all, if the kids at school could hear Zen's incredible voice, maybe they would accept him the way the people at SSC did.

"I'm sorry, but it's not possible, not in the least," declared Zen.

"*Why not?*" Rebecca and I asked at the same time.

I couldn't believe he wouldn't grab at this opportunity to prove himself, to speak louder than the Sachem Regional crowd.

"Because as soon as they see me, they'll hate whatever comes out of my mouth."

I looked at Rebecca and she looked down at her lap. I didn't know what to say. He was probably right.

Out of nowhere Babs yelled, "Wear a disguise!" Then she cackled like a witch and made a giant swerve around a bicyclist. My stomach did somersaults.

"Forget it," said Zen. "Just as the great musical legend Florence Ballard stood up to those studio executives in Detroit, I too refuse to be anyone other than myself. No disguises, ever."

"Who's Florence Ballard?" asked Rebecca.

Zen sighed. "Doesn't anyone listen to Motown anymore?"

"That's it!" I cried.

Zen jumped. "What's what?"

"You can wear a disguise *and* be true to yourself in the Musical Medley!" I exclaimed. "Instead of dressing and acting like Middle School Zen, conform and sing like Seacoast Spiritual Zen."

Pop had laid out a variety of toppings for the pizza. I chose ballpark sausage and extra cheese. Rebecca combined mushrooms, peppers, and onions. Mom had already made a Greek pizza with feta and black olives.

"Would you happen to have pickles in the fridge, Mr. Bunt?" inquired Zen. "I like the intensity of dill with the tomato sauce."

"You're a man after my own heart," said Pop, who put anything and everything on his pizza.

Throughout lunch Rebecca and I continued to pester

Zen about singing in the Musical Medley.

"If you wore your nice blue shirt, your dark pants, maybe some sunglasses, and parted your hair without crimping it," I said, "no one in the audience would even recognize you."

"But you'd still be you," added Rebecca.

"The *true* you."

"And you could sing a really cool song."

"With your church voice."

"And Alice and I would cheer as loudly as we can."

Zen couldn't fight his smile. He shifted in his seat. He whined. He groaned. He scratched his back. He sighed.

"When is it?" he finally asked.

I chewed my lip anxiously. "Saturday."

"You don't mean this coming Saturday!" exclaimed Zen. "Six-days-from-now Saturday?"

I nodded. "I think auditions are tomorrow after school."

Zen slid as far down in the chair as he could without falling on the floor. I glanced at my parents, looking for help, but they only smiled.

"Oh, Zen!" Rebecca begged. "We promise we'll go to the audition with you."

Just then Yaz meowed and jumped on Zen's lap.

"See, even Yaz wants you to do it."

"He probably wants a can of sardines," said Zen.

I had to laugh. I was so relieved that we were real friends again, even better friends than before.

Zen took a deep breath and made his squishy face. "I guess it can't hurt too much to just audition."

Rebecca and I squealed and jumped up and down.

"But that doesn't mean I'll *definitely* do it."

We sat down and squealed a little more quietly.

"Let's go back to your house," I suggested, "and think of a really amazing song for you to sing."

"Not necessary, Sister Alice," said Zen. He held up his hands like we were back at his church. "I know, without a question, which song I shall perform. A personally spiritual song, close to my heart."

chapter twenty·two

The next morning I was fretting so much I chewed my fingernails, which I had never done before. As we sat in homeroom, Rebecca said something about the Musical Medley, but I didn't hear a word. I was still in shock. I couldn't believe that Zen was actually planning to sing a Sacred Circle song in a middle-school talent show.

I knew it had been my idea for him to perform as the Seacoast Spiritual Zen, but only in appearance. It had never occurred to me that he would actually sing *or chant* one of those strange earth-based hymns! I wondered if it was against the law to sing a religious song in a public school.

"Are you all right?" asked Rebecca. She lightly shook my shoulder.

"I think we made a colossal mistake."

"What are you talking about?"

"If Zen sings an SSC song," I whispered, "while everyone else performs the Top 40, he'll be laughed back to grade school."

"But it's his choice, Alice," said Rebecca, readjusting her glasses. "He has to sing what he feels like singing."

At lunch, Zen was in a great mood, which was emphasized by his colorful outfit—a Mexican smock over white jeans and sandals.

"I consulted my chart last night," he confessed, wriggling in his seat.

He slipped a small meatloaf out of its small pan and ate it carefully with his hands. Watching him made my stomach twist into those now familiar middle-school knots. How could I talk him out of auditioning? I couldn't eat my sandwich.

"What kind of chart?" asked Rebecca.

"My astrological chart. I'm a Scorpio." His mouth was half full. "My horoscope said that I'll discover new meaning in my life this week and not to be afraid, but to march bravely forward."

"The Musical Medley!" said Rebecca.

"Exactly," answered Zen. He took another bite of his mini-meatloaf and asked, "When is your birthday?"

"June eighth," replied Rebecca. "I'm a Gemini."

"That would make sense," commented Zen. "You're open-minded, playful, quick."

Rebecca asked, "What about you, Alice?"

"April seventeenth," I muttered unenthusiastically. I was racking my brain trying to figure out what to do.

"No wonder you're a leader, Alice!" said Zen, wiping his face with a yellow napkin. "Aries are naturally charismatic."

I wasn't feeling very charis—whatever it was he said I was.

Just then Haley and Yvette strutted over with their crowd.

"Hey Alice! I hear your *freak* friend is auditioning for the Musical Medley," Haley yapped, pointing a manicured finger at Zen.

"Why would you care, Haley?" I asked without looking up.

"Actually *we* care very much," she replied.

"Yeah," added Yvette.

Zen was turning redder by the second. Rebecca pinched my leg and shook her head, warning me to ignore them.

"We can't wait to see him make an even bigger fool of himself," said Haley, "when he loses to us, the Hip-Hop Hotties!"

Yvette and the other girls posed, then exploded into laughter. They waltzed across the cafeteria to their table like they owned the place. Zen slumped over his food.

"Don't listen to them," said Rebecca. "They have no idea what they're talking about. Haley can't even whistle."

"But she's right," mumbled Zen. "They'll probably win anyway."

All of a sudden, that explosion of determination returned. I didn't care how strange he was or whether he wanted to sing about the goddess of sunbeams or the prince of moonbeams. Zen *had* to prove those girls wrong. I knew it would be a long shot, but he had to try.

I grabbed his wrists and yanked him forward. His eyes practically popped out of his head.

"Listen to me. Rebecca's right!" I said firmly. "When you sing on Saturday night, Haley Benson and the rest of this school will be in for the shock of their lives!"

Unfortunately, my astrological powers did not affect the audition sign-up sheet. Zen had filled out the Musical Medley form at the last minute in homeroom that morning. Since he had done it so late, his name was at the end of the audition list, which was taped beside the auditorium doors.

"We'll go in there and wait with you if it takes all day," I said.

Rebecca added, "We've already missed the bus. We can hang around and do homework."

Zen shook his head and took one of his deep cleansing breaths.

"It's okay. I want do this alone. I'll call you both later

and let you know how it goes."

Even though he was trying to smile I noticed he looked queasy, like he might get sick.

"But Zen," I touched his arm. "Haley and Yvette and lots of other really mean kids will be—"

"Alice," he interrupted me, taking another giant breath. "I've had to deal with those people all my life. This time won't be any different."

Chapter twenty-three

"You made it!"

The three of us were standing in front of the lobby bulletin board a couple of minutes before the homeroom bell. As Rebecca and I scanned the list, Zen faced the wall and covered his eyes.

"Are you sure?"

He refused to look at the list.

"Positive!" said Rebecca.

"Maybe you're reading it wrong."

"Do you know anyone else named Zen?" I asked.

He split his fingers and leaned toward the board. He made a squishy face.

"Where am I?"

"Right there," I answered. "The last name."

"That figures," he replied and finally looked.

"You were the last one to try out," said Rebecca.

"That's why you're at the end."

The three of us read the small print, which stated: *The Annual Middle School Musical Medley is free to the public and will take place Saturday, October 8th, at 7:00 p.m. First, Second, and Third Place ribbons will be awarded by our faculty judges. The Grand Prize winner, selected by the audience, will receive a trophy and an all-expenses-paid trip to Boston. For more information, contact Mr. Lewis in the gymnasium.*

The homeroom bell rang.

"See you at lunch!" Rebecca and I called out to Zen.

We had to rush so that we wouldn't receive tardy slips. But Zen lagged behind. He had the same queasy expression as the day before, right before the audition.

"Do you think he's coming down with something?" I asked Rebecca.

"I wouldn't worry," she replied. "I'm sure he'll be fine."

But I wasn't so sure. In fact, he never showed up for lunch. And since Rebecca and I were Zen's only friends, there was no one we could ask what happened to him. At the end of the day, we rushed to the bus, but Zen never got on. I promised Rebecca I would call her as soon as I found out what was wrong.

When the bus finally pulled up to the corner of Hemlock Trail, there was Zen. He was sitting on his ratty lounge chair under the huge, old tree, whose leaves were now dark yellow. As usual, he was reading a magazine and drinking lemonade with ice.

"Where have you been?" I asked. "We were worried."

The autumn air was a bit nippy, but you would never know it by looking at Zen, who was wearing tattered shorts.

"Here," he said. "Wanna take a quiz on your personality traits?"

"No, I want to know why you left school today."

"Actually, this test tells you precisely why."

"Zen," I said, "I don't want to take a magazine quiz."

"Well, I took it, and you know what my personality traits are?"

I grabbed the magazine.

"I don't need a quiz to tell me who you are. They only make these dumb things up so people like you will buy them, and then they get big companies to advertise in them so you'll buy their dumb products too!"

Zen didn't say anything. He stared down at his lemonade and blew bubbles with his straw. I pulled the dirty beach chair over and sat next to him. An acorn hit my head. I looked up.

"What kind of tree is this anyway?"

Before answering, Zen deliberately finished his drink slowly and then placed the glass carefully on the ground.

"This tree happens to be the oldest living oak tree in Oakville. As a matter of fact, I believe it's older than every single thing in this town."

Now that he mentioned it, it was the biggest tree I had ever seen.

"When the developers came in and plowed down every last hemlock to tar your road, they *begged* Babs and me nearly every day to sell our property. Something about building a fancy gate right across our yard with the words *Hemlock Estates*. Can you imagine? Not only were they going to level our beloved home, but they were going to chop down the oldest oak tree in Oakville, maybe even in America, just to erect a pompous sign!"

I watched Zen drink his lemonade and thought about what he'd said. It seemed it had been hard for him to hang on to just about everything important in his life.

I opened the magazine and flipped through the pages.

"Okay. So what are your personality traits?" I asked.

Silence.

"Zen? The quiz?"

"*Not* a risk-taker," he finally replied, staring at his flip-flops. "Fearful, timid, weak, cowardly. My horoscope was all wrong."

"It's not true," I said. "You *are* brave. You're probably the bravest person I know."

And he *was*. He bravely wore peculiar outfits. For weeks he sat in the cafeteria, bravely eating lunch alone. He bravely reported a student for cheating, even though he knew the kid would punch him in the nose. And most of all, he bravely faced each day without a mother or father.

He glanced at me sideways while chewing on his straw.

"If I'm so brave, why do I gag every time I think of that horrid Musical Medley contest?"

"You got through the audition," I pointed out.

"That was the easy part," he said. "I was last, so no one was there but Mr. Lewis!"

I took a minute to think.

"I guess this contest will be the scariest thing you've ever done," I finally replied. "It probably feels like standing in front of everyone without any clothes on."

He grinned.

"But you have to try, Zen."

He blew some more lemonade bubbles.

"Why?"

"So that you'll be"—I looked for the right word—"accepted."

"They'll never accept me at school."

I thought about what Pop had said.

"They might if they hear your true voice."

I handed the magazine back to him.

"I'll take that quiz now."

Zen's face lit up like a jack-o-lantern. He quickly found the page and asked each question as if my answers would unlock the mysteries of the universe.

It turned out my personality traits were loyal, predictable, stable, solid. I guess there was a little truth to some of those magazine tests, but I wasn't about to admit that to him.

chapter twenty-four

Before I knew it, it was Saturday night.
Rebecca and I went to the Musical Medley together.
By seven o'clock the auditorium was filled to capacity.
The crowd was already cheering and clapping as if the
voting had begun.

I was so nervous. Would Zen go through with the
show? I'd wanted to convince him to do it, but now
that the moment was here, I realized it was his decision
to make. Not mine.

All of a sudden, the lights went down. A hush fell
over the crowd. Mr. Lewis marched to the center of the
stage as if preparing to fight a duel.

"Settle down, settle down!" he bellowed.

But the audience made more noise, so he lifted his
coach's whistle and blew it as hard as he could.

"Let's get started, people, or we'll be here all night!"

Silence.

I glanced at Rebecca. She rolled her eyes and giggled.

"Now, welcome to the Musical Medley competition. Remember, our faculty judges will select first, second, and third place. But *your* applause will determine the grand-prize winner, who, in addition to a trophy, will be awarded a fancy trip to Boston."

There was some more cheering, so Mr. Lewis blew his whistle again.

"I don't want to have to keep using this thing!" he hollered at the crowd.

Finally, everyone calmed down.

"Okay, let's get a move on it and welcome our first group. Give it up, folks, for the Hip-Hop Hotties!"

Haley and Yvette were totally terrible. There was absolutely nothing musical about their act. For the most part they did cheerleading jumps. Occasionally they moved their mouths, lip-syncing the song. And their three backup girls shuffled and bumped into each other between fits of nervous laughter. I almost felt badly for them until the audience burst into applause and then a standing ovation.

I began to really worry.

What if Zen was right, and the Medley was nothing more than a popularity contest? What if he went ahead with his performance and got booed off the stage? Maybe I'd been wrong about how people would accept him if he showed his true voice. What if they totally rejected him in front of the entire school?

There were so many acts I lost count somewhere between the Country-Western Corndogs and the Rockin' Sock'em Tree Stumps. Like Haley and Yvette, most of them were awful. Some were so horrible they were comical. A couple of the contestants, like the eighth-grade violinist, were great. But of course, they were the ones who received the least applause.

At last, Mr. Lewis swaggered to the center of the stage to announce the twentieth and final act.

My heart was beating so hard. I covered my eyes as if I were watching a super-scary movie.

"I have to say, gang," shouted Mr. Lewis, "this last act is a doozy."

I dropped my hands. Rebecca and I looked at each other in disbelief. For a second, I wasn't sure what he meant.

"One of the best talents *I've* seen in years!"

"Wow," I whispered. "Is he talking about Zen?"

Suddenly, Rebecca nudged me in the ribs. At the far end of the stage, there he was, peering around the edge of the curtain, searching the sea of faces. Immediately, I popped up and snuck down the outside aisle toward him.

"Now, folks," continued Mr. Lewis, "here's an example of a young individual who is very talented, but I bet not one of you even knows that."

"Zen," I whispered from below the stage. "You're here!"

"Oh Alice, I'm going to be sick!"

Only his head was sticking out from around the curtain, but I noticed his hair was parted on the side. It looked nice.

"But didn't you hear what Mr. Lewis just said about you? He thinks you're fantastic!"

"I don't care, Alice," Zen hissed. "I don't think I can do this!"

"Now don't let *me* influence your vote!" yelled Mr. Lewis, a little too loudly. Then he pointed at the audience. "You be the judge."

My mind quickly flipped through everything I had learned in the last couple of months.

"Zen, you know what? You don't have to do this."

"Really?" He looked completely relieved.

"But remember, *you* were the one who taught me how to walk to the music in my head—and not to the music of the Hip-Hop Hotties. So I know you can do this if you really want to. But only if *you* want to do it."

I didn't wait for him to respond. There was nothing more to say and I was out of time. I rushed back to my seat just as Mr. Lewis shouted his introduction.

"*Sooooo*, let me present to you Oakville's grooviest singer! Give a big round of applause for MISTER MOTOWN!"

Mr. Motown? I smiled to myself. So that's what Zen meant when he said he'd sing a personally spiritual song, close to his heart.

The curtains parted and the crowd exploded into applause. Rebecca and I clapped louder than anyone. In the back row a bunch of people whistled and screamed. The stage was dark, but I could tell it was still empty.

Rebecca grabbed my hand.

"Is he going to do it?" she whispered.

I had no idea.

Finally, the cheering died down. Then a figure tiptoed through the shadows and stood in the center of the stage in front of the microphone. By now my heart was pounding so hard, my hands were shaking.

As the lights came up slowly, I could tell Zen's eyes were closed. He started to sway a little at first, then harder. We could hear him hum the tune. He nodded his head and tapped his foot. His whole body was moving to the beat, but he still wasn't singing.

Just then, normally shy Rebecca leapt to her feet, clapping and stomping along with the rhythm, as if we were back at the Seacoast Spiritual Center. I jumped up and did the same. And then the people way in the last row joined us.

Zen finally opened his eyes and his mouth. And to my amazement—in front of the entire middle school, his shoulders pulled back and his head held high—Zenithal Stevie Wonder Malinowski belted out the very music he heard in his head every time he walked.

He was brave. He was original. He was truly Zenithal.

chapter twenty five

"You won! You won! You WON!"

Rebecca and I charged Zen in the lobby, where everyone was waiting for the contestants. We grabbed him on either side.

"Oh my gosh!" he said, passing around his third-place ribbon. "It's a miracle!"

He was clammy and flushed but beaming ear-to-ear. I noticed he was wearing his SSC dress shirt and dark pants.

As people passed by they called out *Groovy!* and *Hey Mister Motown!* Not one shove or cruel remark or even a frown. Until Haley and Yvette skipped by with the Hip-Hop Hotties—and the trophy.

"We're going to Boston, we're going to Boston!" they sang in unison.

As Zen had predicted, they had won the Grand

Prize . . . but just barely.

Suddenly Haley stopped and stared at me. I took a deep cleansing breath and ignored her. I wasn't about to let her ruin our wonderful moment. Then she turned to Zen.

"Nice pipes, Malinowski," she remarked. "What *was* that song anyway?"

"The Motown classic 'For Once in My Life,' written in 1968 by the legendary singer-songwriter Stevie Wonder, from the album of the same name."

Haley studied him for a few seconds. Then she said, "Cool," and walked away.

Zen made his squishy face as we fell onto each other, giggling uncontrollably.

"Now *that* was a miracle!" he said.

"It most certainly was!"

We all twirled around to identify the source of a deep, smooth voice.

"Wintermoon!" cried Zen. "The Sacred Songsters! You came!"

Standing behind Wintermoon were at least a dozen

people I recognized from the Seacoast Spiritual Center. So they had been the applause and cheers roaring from the back row. I should have known.

"We're only going for three days," I said.

The two of us were sitting in Zen's bedroom about a month after the Musical Medley. Mom and Pop had suggested awarding Zen a popularity prize from us—a weekend in Boston with the Bunts. After all, we were the local experts.

"But what if it suddenly turns cold or windy?" he replied.

As Zen overstuffed his suitcase, I glanced around his bedroom. The Motown posters were neatly retaped, the walls newly painted with a fresh coat of "golden glow." His sacred herbal candles were arranged in small groupings, and he had recycled most of his old magazines. And best of all, the two new shells in his collection were painted yellow. One from Rebecca and a special BF shell from me.

After all, a person can have more than one best friend.

Zen started rooting around his closet again.

"Oh my gosh, I can't forget my umbrella!"

It was the middle of November and overcast.

"Zen, are you still allergic to the sun this time of year?"

"Not as much, but what if it rains?"

I helped him drag his suitcase out the door and down the hall. It was stiff and old-fashioned, the kind my grandparents still used.

"So long, Babs!" called Zen. "There's lasagna in the freezer and dumpling stew in the fridge. And the number of the hotel is by the phone."

"Hazelnuts!" yelled his grandmother. "You just made me miss what Sheriff Andy said to Opie!"

As we made our way up Hemlock Trail, Zen talked about his latest issue of *Body by Design*, which featured real estate in California. He said he needed to start saving now if he was going to open up a total body salon after college. As he babbled about his plans, I whistled my fave song, "Take Me Out to the Ball Game." I let my arms swing and my hips sway as I walked to the beat of my very own music.

Even though the sky was gray, it was a warm day for November. Up ahead in the cul-de-sac, our neighbors were outside enjoying the last days of fall. The quads were rollerskating into one another. The Lees were arguing in their garage as Kissy-Missy yapped through the living room window. Mrs. Reed, her stomach much bigger now, was sitting on her wooden lawn chair, smiling at nothing, while Mr. Reed raked up the last of the autumn leaves. And Travis was driving my go-kart around and around the circle for the hundredth time that week.

In our yard, Mom and Pop stood by the minivan waiting for us. Ready to go. Holding Yaz and Einstein. They waved, Zen and I waved back . . . and I thought to myself, this life is going to be pretty perfect after all.

about the author

Elizabeth Atkinson has been an editor, a children's librarian, an English teacher, and a newspaper columnist. *From Alice to Zen and Everyone in Between* is her first novel. She lives in West Newbury, Massachusetts. Readers can learn more about her work at www. elizabethatkinson.com.